FAMILY

FAMILY

THE GIRL IN THE BOX
BOOK FOUR

Robert J. Crane

FAMILY

THE GIRL IN THE BOX, BOOK FOUR

Robert J. Crane
Copyright © 2012
All Rights Reserved.

Contact Robert J. Crane via email at
cyrusdavidon@gmail.com

Layout provided by **Everything Indie**
http://www.everything-indie.com

Acknowledgments

Whenever I put one of these books out, I'm always afraid I'm going to mess it up by failing to mention someone who deserves it. Writing the book may be a solitary effort, done in a locked room after chaining myself to the keyboard, but the state it comes out in is one that is totally unfit for print, a disaster of epic proportions filled with grammatical errors, misspellings and failures of continuity both minute and massive. To my editorial squad of beta readers, I give thanks:

Shannon Garza, for not only fixing the grammar and spelling, but helping me to improve flow and clarity, and keeping Sienna on the correct emotional keel.

Robin McDermott for letting me know when I was getting too "wordy." Or as I would put it before she corrected it, "diffuse." She also caught lots of other errors, but this is what I get the biggest kick out of, reading her notes.

Calvin Sams always does a readthrough and provides notes, and this time is no different. Thanks, Calvin, for keeping an eye out for me!

Damarra Atkins focused on the geek aspects, as she is well attuned to geek culture and managed to even pick up on some of the more obscure references in the manuscript. And that is why I have left them in; so long as one person gets them, they stay.

Debra Wesley once more kept an eye on the technical aspects of the manuscript, letting me know when things don't quite work the way I think they do. I know I write fantasy, but that's no excuse for a complete departure from any sort of reality, and Deb keeps these books grounded nicely.

And what can I say about Heather Rodefer that hasn't already been said? She's the nicest Packer fan I've ever encountered, and I mean that in as complimentary a fashion as possible coming from a Minnesotan to a Wisconsinite. She is the error correction patrol, the final authority when it comes to mistakes in the manuscript. Without her, I shudder to think what horror I would be producing, and I know it would not be fit for public consumption.

Once again the cover of this work has been created by the excellent Karri Klawiter of Artbykarri.com, who I can't say enough nice things about. She's great to work with and always seems to come up with a fantastic idea for the covers.

The final editing duties were handled once more by Nicholas J. Ambrose of everything-indie.com. In addition to being a superb Halo player he can also fix a manuscript in record time, then make it beautifully presentable in every e-format known to humanity. And all this just weeks after Halo 4 came out – this makes him quite the wonder.

Last of all, it seems appropriate that in a book titled Family that I take an extra moment to thank mine. My extended family has been ridiculously supportive of my career, far beyond what I could have expected and miles better than what I've heard of other authors in similar situations. Thank you all.

Also, thanks to my mom and dad, and my kids, who have given me both the tools and the reason to use them in this field of endeavor I have chosen.

I've heard it put in better terms than mine that "faith is the evidence of things not seen." My wife had faith in me when there was literally nothing to see, and believed in me enough to back my crazy play to be an independent author back when it made zero sense to anyone but me. For that (and much more), I am eternally grateful.

Chapter 1

One Year Earlier

I was sitting on the couch watching a stupid sitcom when she came out of her bedroom. There were times I could tell Mom was on edge, ready to pick a fight, and that was one. "You didn't clean my bathroom," she said. I ignored her the first time. Don't know why I did it; it's not like ignoring her had ever stopped her before.

She walked across the living room. The darkness from all the windows being covered was kept at bay by the lamps I had on. The dull flicker of our TV (an old, square boxy one, not the new, flat HD kind) cast shadows that jumped as it switched between scenes, casting the room in a brighter shade of bluish light. Our brown suede couch was pressed against my cheek, the smoothness of the material felt oddly warm, heating up the side of my face that lay against it. I was stretched out, the hot dogs I had eaten for dinner making me sluggish and sleepy, the smell still hanging in the air from an hour ago when I had microwaved them.

Our house was small, and the main living area was over half of the first floor. Mom didn't even have to shout to be heard over the television, standing only ten feet away from me, at the entrance to the hallway that led to the bedrooms. "Sienna. You didn't clean…" she said, forcing my eyes to come to her for a moment before they went back to the TV, "…my bathroom."

"I'll get it once my show is over," I said, uncaring. On the screen, Neil Patrick Harris was propositioning a woman, and I wanted to see if she'd fall for his line of bull or not. I suspected she would; fictional women were prone to being blindsided by jerks who just wanted to get in their pants. I knew this because I watched an hour of TV a day and read copious amounts of books, and there was a distinct common theme when it came to most of the women I saw – get used, abused, and discarded. Bleh.

She took another step, blocking the TV, casting her shadow over me, her silhouette outlined by the light from the screen. "You'll do it now."

"Hey!" I sat up, all thoughts of laziness and lying on the couch evaporated, the heat already in my face from irritation.

"Your chores aren't done," she said, a smug, self-satisfied look on her face. "Clean the bathroom and you can finish watching it."

I glanced at the clock. "It'll be over by the time I get done cleaning," I said, and pointed at the digital clock on the microwave. We didn't own a DVR, those magical things I'd heard others talking about – on TV, only. I hadn't left my house for as long as I could remember.

"Then I bet next time you want to watch a show you'll make sure your chores are done before I get home," she said, and her smile was overly sweet, patronizing.

"Really?" I asked, my studied disbelief allowing me to keep a calm I didn't feel inside. "You're that bent out of shape about me failing to do one little chore that you want me to shut off the TV ten minutes before the end of my show?

"No," she said, and there was an undercurrent in the way she said it that caused my muscles to tense involuntarily. "I don't want you to shut off the TV." She reached down and pushed the power button on the front of the unit, and it flipped off in a flash that seemed almost in slow motion as it disappeared into a pinprick of light at the center of the screen. "I'll take care of it for you."

"What the—" I was on my feet in a quarter second. "I was watching that!" I knew my voice was raised; dangerous ground. I didn't care.

"Now you're not," she said. "If you want to be watching it again, go clean the bathroom."

"It's not my fault you shed hair like a cat," I said, not bothering to keep my voice down. "I shouldn't have to clean up your mess!"

Her eyebrows tilted down, and I knew I was edging onto her nerves. Good. "Cleaning my bathroom, as well as yours, is something you clearly know to be part of your weekly responsibilities. This is not new. It has occurred every week for years, and is not something you simply forget and do later – it is something that you pretend to forget every so often, because you find it unpleasant. That's a shame," she said without any remorse. "But as an adult I find all sorts of things I do unpleasant, such as working to pay for your housing, your clothes, the food you eat, the television you enjoy—"

"When I abide by your tyrannical commands."

"When you follow *the rules*," she said, slow, steady, the cadence of the words drumming into my head. "When you do *as I say*. You need to learn responsibility to accompany your self-discipline, and it's as important as any martial art I could teach you."

"I don't care about any of the things you want to teach me," I said, and I heard a hiss in the back of my throat, like air escaping from an overinflated ball.

"That's not a luxury you're afforded," she said, the faintest hint of dark clouds beginning to gather around her head. I was steaming, though, and I wanted to push; I could feel the heat boiling off my skin. "You're edging closer and closer to testing the boundaries," she said. "Do you need a reminder of what happens when you push the limits in this house?"

"What limits?" I snapped back. "Nothing is allowed in this house! Oh, wow, I get an hour of TV per day after all my schoolwork and chores and if I haven't offended the warden! Wow, that hour of TV really makes my other twenty-three worth living; it's a standard of living one step above life in a French prison a couple centuries ago."

"If you'd like, I can take away your TV and your copy of 'The Man in the Iron Mask' as well," my mom snarked. "Then you wouldn't have a frame of comparison for the tragic cruelties of your life, and maybe you'd realize that you've got a bed to sleep in and enough food to eat, somewhere warm to live, and safety from all the other dangers you don't even know exist out in the world—"

"Because you won't let me out in the world to see." I glared at her. "It's all a big mystery, and when you walk out the door every day and shut it behind you so I can't see what's going on, you leave me here in the dark – unless we're talking about the times you lock me in the box, because then you REALLY leave me in the dark—"

"Someday you'll understand," she said, a fire taking over in her, her hair bobbing as she shook her head. "Someday you'll see, and realize how lucky you were I protected you all these years, kept you safe, even if you don't like the way I do it—"

"You always say that, you self-righteous bitch!" I let it fly before I could stop myself. My shoulders and chest heaved with the reckless emotion. Mother blanched almost imperceptibly. "Protect me from what? Keep me safe from what? You won't tell me, you won't say a damned word about what it is that you're saving me from. You just throw me in a metal box in order to keep me here," I gestured at the walls around us, "in this box so we can't talk about what goes on outside it—"

"We don't discuss what happens outside these walls," she almost hissed.

"I'm talking about what happens inside them," I said. "About you locking me in. Unless it's all a desolate, post-apocalyptic world outside, you're keeping me away from something." I smiled in small triumph. "You can't keep me in here forever, Mother. Someday—"

She moved fast, faster even than she did when we would spar in the basement while she taught me martial arts. "Not today," she said, her face a mask and her hand gripping my upper arm, pinching into the flesh and causing me to cry out as she jerked me off-balance. "And I've had enough of your smart mouth, your casual disdain, your insolence—"

"And I've had enough of you!" I yelled, and she jerked my arm again, dragging me along behind her toward the basement. "I hate you! I hate you!"

I couldn't see her face, but her dark hair swayed as she pulled me down the steps. I tried to resist, and halfway down I caught the railing. She pulled me so hard my sweaty fingers slipped off of it and my knee hit the floorboard. I felt the skin tear and cried out, but she never stopped. I was forced back to my feet as she half-walked, half-carried me down the stairs. When we reached the landing I tried to pull away again. I could feel the tears coursing down my cheeks, partly from rage, partly from the humiliation of having my whole person violated by being treated so roughly. I could feel the trickle of blood running down my shin under my pants.

"Someday you'll realize," she said, dragging me around in front of her as she stopped at the foot of the wooden stairs, "all this is for you."

"I don't care about someday! I hate you!"

"So be it," she said, unflinching, unreacting, emotionless. "But you will still respect me – and the rules. And you will obey."

She twisted my arm again and I cried out as she pulled me the last few steps toward the box. It stood a hair over six feet in height, metal, a couple feet deep and a few feet wide – big enough to imprison me easily enough – and with enough space that I could slide to my haunches and sit with my knees folded in front of me, so I could rest my head on them and fall asleep. "I'll never respect you," I said. "I hate you and I always will."

"Fine," she said, her voice iron. She pushed me into the box, and I hit the back and felt it wobble, as though it would tilt and fall over, leaving me on my back. My eyes widened but she stepped in and stabilized it with one foot, returning it to equilibrium. I had tipped it before, in the past, and it was horrible, being stuck laying flat. I preferred it the way it was, end up, and she knew it. "Don't push me, Sienna," she said, holding me inside. I saw her eyes, and there was something else in there, something deep, behind the irises, something beyond fire or anger. She shut the door and I heard the pin secure it – there was no escape, not now. "And I won't push you," she said through the small, mailslot-like hole that hovered in front of my face.

"I'm sorry," I said, not really sorry but realizing at last, as my fury abated, that this was not where I wanted to be. "I'm sorry! Please, let me out!"

"You should spend your time in there thinking about how you'll do things differently when you get out," she said, her inflection dull, dead, as bored as if she were doing something menial that required no thought. Cleaning the bathroom, perhaps. "We won't have this happen again."

"I hate you," I said, and I sobbed, and realized I hated myself for doing it, for showing this measure of weakness. "I wish my father were here. He would have loved me. He wouldn't have ever done any of this to me. Not like you, you f—"

"Your father would understand," she said, acknowledging the man even existed for only the second time since I'd known her. "This – all of this – it's for your own—"

"You don't care anything about my good," I said sullenly, and stared back at her eyes. "You don't care about me at all."

She stared at me again, a long, uninterrupted silence between us, and I thought I caught just a waver, that certain something in her eyes, as it threatened to break loose. But after a moment it was gone, replaced by the implacable look of Mother, just as she was every time I went in – undeterred. "It'd be easier to think that's true," she said, voice husky. "But if it was, I'd let you out. You need to learn. Following the rules will save your life. Discipline will save your life."

Her fingers came up and I saw them move through the slot, and it started to slide closed as I held myself together for only the seconds before it was shut, leaving the darkness to surround me. I began to sob, slowly at first, as one made its way out, then another, and another as I started to break down, great heaving emotions causing me to lay my back against the wall of the box and slide down, my arms wrapped around my knees as I sat in the darkness, alone – just like always.

Chapter 2

Now

The rocket-propelled grenade hit our car with the force of a sledgehammer against an egg, waking me out of a sound sleep. We had been on our way back from Eagle River, Wisconsin, and I had fallen asleep. It had been a long day – and night, and several more of those before this one. I don't know when I had passed out, but I knew that most of the sleep I'd had over the last few days had taken place in hotel rooms and cars, and I was lucky that I had abilities to heal that were above normal humans, because otherwise I would have had a permanent crick in my neck.

I felt the shock of the explosion reverberate through my head as the car, already swerving, was lifted from the ground and went into a sideways roll. I felt my body jerk to the side, my head hitting the window it had been resting against, breaking it as the roof crumpled above me as it hit the road.

Everything seemed to be at half speed, as though I could see the fragments of glass rush in front of my eyes in slow motion, pelting Andromeda, who sat next to me, and Scott Byerly, who was in the seat beside her at the other window. I saw Zack and Kurt in front of us, their heads jerked to the right by the motion of the car flipping, Zack's hands still anchored on the steering wheel.

The car came upright again, all four tires exploding from the force of our landing. My seatbelt held me tight, snug against the soft leather interior, and my head smacked the headrest. When I blinked away the feeling of disorientation, I realized that the front of the car was smoking at the hood, and the windshield was broken, only shards left, like little pebbles all stacked together around the edges of the window.

It was Scott who spoke first, bleariness heavy in his voice. "What. The. Hell. Did we just set a record by hitting the world's largest roadkill?"

I felt a stinging pain on my forehead, and when my hand reached up, I felt sticky blood, and my fingers came away with crimson adhering to the whorls of my fingerprints. "Roadkill doesn't explode when you hit it," I said. "That was an RPG."

"Again?" Scott asked. "How many is that today?"

"Don't stop to count now," I said, fumbling for my seatbelt. "I wouldn't want you to strain yourself when you should be fleeing for your life."

"Do you...ever..." Kurt was talking from in front of me, but his voice was a rasp. "Just...get serious...for a minute?" I released my seatbelt and leaned forward, looking over the seat, which was tilted at a funny angle. Kurt was arched forward, pinned against the dash, and blood was running out of his mouth. His airbag had deployed but had already deflated, looking like a used white t-shirt that hung from above the glove box, and he was mashed against it.

"Never," I said, and clicked the release for his seatbelt. There was smoke in the air, a chemical aroma that made me want to gag. And something else, too, as I turned my head to look at Zack. "Are you okay?"

"Who, me?" He shook his head, and slapped at his airbag, which was still inflated. "My car just got hit by rocket fire on a rural Wisconsin highway. I'm pretty damned far from okay." His hands ran along the length of his body, as though he were checking for injuries. "But I think I'm uninjured, for the most part." He kicked his door open and started to get out.

"I am also fine," I heard Andromeda say behind me. "But the one behind me did not fare quite so well." I looked back at Andromeda, wondering what she meant by that. Her sandy hair looked different than when I had met her, now that it was dry. She wore a tourist T-shirt that we had bought in Eagle River that had the name of the town etched on it along with a picturesque landscape reflective of that area of the northwoods, along with sweat pants.

I realized after a moment what she meant, and I cringed. "Scott, check on Reed." I saw the blond man nod, and then lean over the seat to get to Reed, who had been sitting in the hatchback when we flipped.

"Not good," Scott said as I tried to open my door and failed. "He's hurt pretty bad."

I breathed a curse, then kicked the door open, breaking it free of its hinges and sending it skidding across the pavement. I heard a noise in the distance, over the crackling of the flames that were beginning to grow under the hood of the car, a slow, steady, repetitive noise that sounded like the humming of tires against pavement when you're in a car driving down the highway.

I knew, though, when I stepped out of the car, that it wasn't that. The cadence was too high; it was cycling far too fast to be anything of that sort. It was something else, something that spun at a much faster rate than tires, something that was disturbing the air around it rather than beating against unrelenting asphalt. A helicopter overflew us, one of the old Hueys like the ones from Vietnam war movies, and it settled into a slow descent only a hundred yards in front of us.

The highway we had been on had two lanes, with woods running along either side past the small ditches that were placed below the sides of the road to catch runoff. There were buildings a mile behind us, a small town built on the highway, and there were a few mailboxes spaced out on the shoulder. One was only fifty feet from where I stood. "Mailboxes mean houses," I said under my breath.

"They are no safe haven," Andromeda said, slipping out of

the car behind me to take up position at my side.

"We need to get these guys out of here," I told her as I watched the helicopter continue its descent; the only thing slowing it was the power lines that ran along either side of the road. "Any house will do for now; at least it's cover."

Scott came around the crumpled side of the car, Reed on his back in a fireman's carry. He passed the side where black paint was so streaked with gray scratches that the steel peeked out from underneath. It looked like it had been keyed by the most pissed-off ex-girlfriend ever. "They've got RPGs and no reluctance to use them; I expect they'll blow the roof off a house in short order."

I looked at him for only a second as I ripped Kurt's door off. "Are you sure you should be moving him like this?"

Scott tried to shrug, a vain effort given Reed was draped over his shoulders. "Move them or leave them for the guys with guns and rockets."

"They will not show mercy," Andromeda said. "They have none in them." Her brown eyes were distant, and I followed them along a line to the helicopter, which had landed and was starting to deploy men in black, at least six of them, their dark outfits making them look like ninjas, covered from head to toe as they were. Cars were backing up behind the helicopter, a small traffic jam forming thanks to their deployment.

"Sienna's right. We go for cover and worry about how flimsy it is afterward," Zack said, startling me as he came around the front of the car, speaking to me through the flames on the engine. The air was filling with acrid smoke, causing me to gag from the smell of it. He chucked his thumb at the military-style team that had begun to move toward us. "We're not going to get help from the Directorate for a while, so we need to move." He pulled his pistol and extended it in the direction of our attackers, who were closing. "No time for debate."

"What about Jackson and Hodgkins?" Scott asked, referring

to the agents that had been riding with us until we had gotten to Wausau, where we had dropped them off to rent a car.

"Probably an hour behind us," Zack said. "Ariadne gave us orders to floor it to get home; they were supposed to obey the speed limits."

"Kurt," I said, changing the subject. "He's hurt bad, but I can free him if you give me a few minutes."

"No time," Zack said, and gave me a gentle push. "We go now without him or we all die."

"Did you call them?" Scott asked, already beginning to run toward the driveway, Reed across his shoulders. "Did you warn the Directorate?"

"I dialed their emergency number," Zack said as we began a sprint toward the driveway. Behind us, I saw the black-clad men, goggles over their eyes. They moved quickly, for humans, but not so fast that I couldn't outrun them.

"You think they'll send M-Squad?" Every step Scott took stirred up dust and dirt as we left the pavement and the highway behind, the trees around us offering a sort of tunnel, lining both sides of the driveway. It felt like a perspective trick, elongating in front of me, stretching out into infinity, as though it would take forever to run it. We had left the fire behind us at the car, but it felt like it was still with us, the stinging smell, the heavy smokiness hanging in the air around me as I ran.

"Doubt it," Zack said. "I think they're still in Kansas. But maybe some agents." He cursed as he hit a low hanging branch at the edge of the driveway. "Hopefully heavily armed!" He said the last words with emphasis, and when Scott shot him a look, he shrugged. "The line is still open; they can hear us at HQ."

"Scott," I said, and he slowed to look at me. "Zack's not going to be able to keep up with us." I felt my resolve harden. "We need to buy him some time."

"How?" Scott shot back at me. "You want to try and stop

some bullets with your face? Or did you forget you're unarmed?"

"Yes," I said, "I forgot that I'm unarmed. Can you try and stop them with your powers?"

"A torrent of water isn't going to slow down a bullet. The only way I could slow them down is by surrendering and making them stop to fill me full of holes."

"I like it," Zack said. "It's got just the air of desperation we're looking for in a plan right now."

The trees thinned ahead as we reached the end of the infinite driveway. The sun brightened overhead as we exploded from under the trees onto an open lawn. The green carpet of grass lay before us, leading to a house set off the driveway. Brown wood siding, a garage tucked neatly under the second floor, it was a rectangular box of a creation. I looked back to see the men in black entering the driveway. Their weapons were raised but they had yet to fire.

I ran, ran like hell, like I would have if Wolfe were nipping at my heels. The only thing holding me back from going all-out was the knowledge that I'd be leaving Zack behind to die, or worse, be scooped up by these Omega bastards and have who-knows-what happen to him. I saw blood staining the leg of his jeans, and it made me pause, slowing my run.

"Into the house?" Scott called back at me.

"Better ideas?" I asked, passing him as I ran up the three short wooden steps to the brown front door. "No? Breaking and entering it is, then."

"Wait!" I heard Zack call as I kicked the door down open. He joined me on the front steps and I heard a little hiss beyond the panting from his run. "We need to be able to shut it," he said.

The first of the shots whistled around me as I stepped to the side of the doorframe to let Scott pass. At least three bullets lodged themselves in the siding above my head, and another broke the glass peephole window of the door. "It's still on the hinges.

Get inside."

I dodged in after Zack, slamming the door and leaning my back against it. Zack had dropped to one knee and was fiddling with the leg of his pants as I yanked open the door of the coat closet to the left of the entry. I grabbed a leather coat from inside and threw it over my uncovered shoulders, my tank top not exactly offering a lot of protection. For others. From my skin.

"They'll surround the house," Zack said, cringing, from the floor. He had lifted his pants leg and I saw blood, lots of it, more than just a superficial cut. I dropped to my knees next to him and his eyes found mine. "You need to get out of here before they do. You guys can get away if you run."

"And leave you behind?" I said, forcing a smile. "I'm pretty sure I just got docked points in a training exercise a few days ago for not working with my team and leaving them behind."

He frowned, and the soft light of the open curtains revealed more pain in his eyes, the skin wrinkled around them. I was reminded, again, of how handsome he was. Even when he ought to look like hell, he didn't – he just looked good. "You left Kurt behind," he said, but the words had no real sting to them.

"You told me we had no choice." I heard someone slam into the door behind me; muffled shouts came from outside.

"You didn't argue."

I blinked away a little excess lubrication of my eyelids. "You're not Kurt."

"I can't keep up, Sienna," he said, and he let his hand brush my cheek. "They're gonna surround the house and come in, and we've got one gun to stop them with. You're all metas." He pointed to Andromeda, then Scott, who was just beyond the living room, standing on the white linoleum in the kitchen. "Our pursuers are human. You can outrun them, easy."

"Probably not their helicopter, though," Scott said, looking around. "Whatever we're going to do, we need to do fast."

"We run," I said, not breaking my eyes off Zack.

"Attagirl," he said with quiet resignation. "Buy time for the Directorate to get here. Do what you have to do."

I felt the emotion rise. "I will." I did it quick, so he wouldn't see it – I raised my hand and clubbed him in the side of the head. Not too hard, but enough that his eyes rolled back. "Sorry," I said as I lifted him onto my shoulders, careful not to touch his skin against mine. "No time for an argument." I turned to Scott. "We go out the back and we run. If they want to come after us with a helicopter, we'll find a big rock and take it out of the damned sky."

"Sounds oddly familiar," Scott said with an ironic smile, leading me out of the entry to the living room and into a kitchen in the back of the house. Andromeda followed us; if she had an opinion, she didn't voice it, but she seemed to be taking everything in. The kitchen was white; linoleum, cabinets, countertops – the whole room felt bright, aided by a floor-to-ceiling sliding glass door that had the shades pulled back from it, the sun illuminating the room.

Sudden motion drew my eyes as Scott adjusted Reed on his shoulders and then lashed out with a kick to the kitchen table, sending it flying through the sliding glass door, breaking it to pieces as the table launched out and flattened two guys in black with submachine guns who had been easing up to it.

I heard the staccato sounds of gunfire pour into the windows on the sides and front of the house and I ran for the sliding glass door, only steps behind Scott. I scooped up one of the submachine guns from one of our fallen attackers, taking a second to stomp his head as I passed. I noticed Scott do the same and we both opened up with bursts of gunfire on the corners of the house as we ran, firing less for effect and more to drive the bastards following us into cover where they wouldn't be able to shoot us – hopefully.

The backyard of the house went several hundred feet to the treeline of the woods behind it. To me it was an open question whether we'd even make it to the woods without getting hit. I vaulted over the cedar railing of the deck, Zack heavy on my shoulders. I heard Andromeda behind me and saw Scott go over as I landed. I ran, feet pounding against the grass. Another burst of gunfire caused me to zag, but it didn't slow me. I turned and fired an offhand three-shot burst that forced a guy behind the corner of the house as I peppered the wall next to him with lead.

I fired another for good measure as I hit the treeline, but this one went wide; I was firing a submachine gun at long range and with one hand; even though I was stronger by far than a human, I wasn't a miracle worker, and the gun kicked quite a bit. I heard bullets pepper the trees over my head, and branches snapped. One hit me in the side of the face as I passed. I veered behind a tree and fired again until the magazine ran dry. I flung the gun as I came over a slight rise and zagged behind another tree, altering my path to give me better cover. A look back confirmed it: I couldn't see the house anymore, the trees allowing me to screen myself from their sight and line of fire.

We ran for minutes, outpacing our pursuers. I could not hear anyone other than Scott, puffing as he ran alongside me, following the natural veer of the landscape. I saw him, his face scratched and slightly bloody from where low-hanging branches had hit him as he passed. Andromeda made not a sound behind us, and I had to look back to make sure she was still there.

The woods were sparse, covered by a layer of dead pine needles, the underbrush not too thick here as we ran down, heading into a natural valley. I saw water in the distance, I thought, though it was hard to tell through the trees and the underbrush.

"Let's go east for a while," Scott said. "Unless there are any objections?"

"None here," I said. "Every direction is the same to me – except for the one we just came from." I looked back to Andromeda, who had stopped about twenty feet behind us, and was holding still, her tourist t-shirt the oddest contrast to her locks of sandy brown. Her face was perfect peace, a contradiction to the way I had met her, screaming, furious. "Andromeda?"

She was staring into the distance, beyond us, and I had started to slow to wait for her. "It doesn't matter," she said softly, and even across the distance between us I understood her words.

"It matters," Scott said, having stopped himself, rebalancing Reed on his shoulder. "We need to get to cover, and find a way to dodge them for a while—"

"Irrelevant," she said. Her eyes were locked on me, and I could see something behind them, something she almost seemed to want to say, but couldn't find the words for.

"Andromeda?" I asked, uncertain. I had stopped, and could hear Scott's breathing behind me. The wind was warm, a little drift of heat running across my face. The breath ran through me, and I could feel Zack's weight on my shoulders, anchoring me to the earth.

"We need to keep moving," Scott said, and I saw him looking around, as though our black-clad pursuers would descend at any moment.

"There is no escape. They have been waiting for this." She seemed so certain, I didn't feel it in me to argue, so I just listened to her. It felt as though all motion had stopped around us, like the woods had frozen, and the sounds of the crickets and birds had ceased, leaving a wall of silence around where we stood in the shade of the forest.

"No time for a defeatist attitude," Scott said. "Let's keep moving."

A gunshot rang out, louder than the submachine guns we had been firing, clear and punctuating. Scott blanched and so did I. I saw Andromeda look down as she fell to her knees. A crimson stain spread outward from the center of her chest, a steady dribble of red running down the front of her white t-shirt. She hit her knees, then fell sideways.

"No," I gasped, and ran to her, felt the rough ground beneath my knees as I landed next to her, dropping Zack without thought or ceremony. "Andromeda," I said, touching her cool skin. I felt a prickle of activity; she had been only one of two people I'd ever met that I could touch without harming, and as my hand landed on her arm, I didn't feel the usual draw of her soul through me, the way I did with others.

It felt…normal? "Andromeda," I said again, cupping her face between my palms.

She let out a breath and coughed, a racking spasm that brought blood to her lips, little drops of it dotting her cheeks and chin, as it came out in a fine mist with every breath and settled on her pale face. She grabbed my arm, pulling me closer, then locked her hands on my face, staring into my eyes. "Remember me, Sienna Nealon," she said, gasping for breath. "Know this…there is a traitor among you, in your Directorate."

"A…what?" Scott said. He was next to me now, watching Andromeda, his eyes wide, his sandy blond hair streaked with dirt and grime from the ground. "A traitor?"

Her eyes flickered open, and she nodded, then focused on me, her brown eyes fading. "Remember me," she said, her eyes still locked on me. "Remember me when you are cast back into the darkness, and I will light your way – I will show you the way." Her next breath brought up more blood, but she smiled through it. She looked up, past me, into the sky. "The sun…haven't seen it…for…"

Her grip on my arm loosed, the light faded from her eyes as she went limp in my arms, the smile disappearing from her face as the muscles went slack.

Chapter 3

"No time to mourn," Scott said, abrupt, a mask of control wavering on his face. "We need to go."

"She's dead," I said, whispering. "She's dead, and—"

"And we're next," Scott said, snapping his fingers in front of me. "You know this. You're the toughest among us. Come on, Sienna, come back to me here. I need you for this. We have to get out of here."

I ran my fingers over Andromeda's neck, thrust them against the skin, pushed hard, hoping for a sign, a pulse, anything. I waited almost ten seconds, but there was nothing. "Okay," I said, and hoisted Zack up on my shoulders. "We go west. We haul ass." I felt my face harden, felt the emotion slip away, behind a wall somewhere, into a box perhaps, in the basement of my mind where I couldn't hear it, where nothing but the slamming of a metal door remained to mark its passage. "And if we can find a way to do so, we kill these bastards – every one of them."

"I don't love our odds here," Scott said. "You think the Directorate is on their way with some help?"

"Possibly," I said, lifting Zack up and taking a step forward, then another, before breaking into a run. "But I wouldn't like to bet my life on them."

"I think you're gonna have to bet your life no matter what. I suspect that helicopter has thermal imaging, and they'll keep tracking us until we find a town or some other way to lose them. Any ideas?" he asked.

"Keep running."

We ran for minutes more, time seeming to stretch as we went.

I tried to focus on taking one breath, one step at a time, tried to put Andromeda out of my mind, along with the thoughts of what would happen next. After a while the scenery ahead changed; I could see the light shining down, the trees ending. "Veer left," I said, and we did, following the treeline down. The chopper was behind us, I could hear it. We continued our run, over hills, through ravines. Every once in a while, it got quiet, and a few minutes later the chopper would fly overhead, sending the two of us scrambling for the nearby trees to hide behind until it passed.

It overflew us again, and ahead I saw daylight. "Woods coming to an end again," Scott said. I could hear the alarm in his voice. I looked right, and knew he was thinking what I was: we had two directions now cut off to us, west and south. "Back the way we came," he said, "either east or north."

"We just came from directly north," I said. "Maybe if we work east for a while—"

The sound of a gun blast sent me to my knees and a sapling a few feet from me exploded into shards of soft wood, snapping in half where the bullet passed through it. "Great; the local lumberjacks are pissed off," I muttered as I tried to get back up.

"When you chop down trees with a .50 cal sniper rifle, I don't think you get to call yourself a lumberjack," Scott said from nearby. "Pretty sure that's against the union bylaws."

"I know this is ironic coming from me," I said, "but this hardly seems the time for bad jokes."

"Sorry," he said, "I didn't know there *was* a time for bad jokes."

"Try the Oscars. There are so many there, no one will even notice."

"You're taking her death well," he said, flat on his belly, looking directly at me.

"I didn't know her well," I said, brushing it aside. "And we're in a life or death situation of our own." I felt the tug of emotions.

"I may cry a little later."

"So you do have feelings," Scott said with a quicksilver grin.

"A few. Don't tell anyone, okay? I might lose my rep around the Directorate as a total badass."

"That's not your reputation," he said, his amusement dying.

I watched him for about a half-second, pondered what he meant, and stopped thinking about it as another shot boomed in my ears. "Think he's getting closer?"

"He doesn't need to," Scott said. "He's got friends. All he needs to do is pin us down while they approach from our sides or back, box us in."

"Envelopment," I said, remembering what Parks had called it when he was instructing us on small-unit combat tactics. "Any ideas for how to get out?"

"My well-oiled mind is failing me at present," he said, rolling onto his back as another shot echoed overhead. "We stand up, they pop us. We belly crawl, they catch us and kill us when they surround us. We surrender..." His voice trailed off, and I thought again about Andromeda, who I had barely known, and I could see by Scott's reaction that he was thinking it too. "What do you think they want?"

"Our heads," I said, pulling Zack's body closer to mine, feeling him snug against my side. "On a pike."

"Oh, good, and here I thought they were only interested in us to harness and enslave our meta-human powers."

"You don't fire a fifty cal at things you don't want dead," I said sadly.

"We're metas; we can take the damage better than a human. They might think we can survive a hit or two."

"Andromeda was a pretty powerful meta," I said. "She didn't."

"You don't know that for fact." He stared back at me, looking across his body, leaves mussed around him. "We had to leave her behind, but she might have healed from that, given time."

"You think so?" I felt a surge of irritation. I hadn't considered that. "You didn't voice it at the time."

"I don't know it's so," he said as another bullet thundered into a maple tree a few feet from us. Loose leaves, stirred by the impact, drifted down to us, one of them landing on Scott's face. He blew it away. "But I needed you to realize we had to leave her behind rather than carry the whole world on our backs while we're trying to escape."

"You ass," I snapped. "What about Zack and Reed? Should we leave them behind, too?"

"If we wanted the best chance to live," Scott said, dirt all over his tanned face, "yes, hypothetically that would have been a good move. Lighter to travel and all that."

"'Hypothetically'?" I said, annoyed, and I heard the sounds of movement in the underbrush around us as the chopper came around again, the blades thrumming in the summer air. I felt the sunshine on my face through the branches overhead.

"It's just a theory," he said, calmer than I was feeling, "and it doesn't look like we'll ever know the answer now."

"Scott."

"Yes?"

I tried to think of the things we'd been through; we'd met when he said some unkind things to me in the cafeteria at the Directorate and followed it up by leaving a nasty note under my door. We hadn't really fought since then, but he'd annoyed me more than once. "You are..." I tried to think of the nice things he'd done for me, and there had been a few. "...an amazing person." I couldn't quite keep the irritation out of my voice, though, and whether it came from the past, the fact that he'd convinced me to leave Andromeda's body behind, or just my aggravation and stress from the fact that I was fairly certain we were going to die in the next few minutes, I couldn't really be sure.

"Your words say 'amazing', but your tone says 'asshole'." He didn't put a lot of spice into his riposte; the first black-clad figure had appeared only a dozen yards away and was easing toward us one slow step at a time. They had us dead to rights, an easy kill. Scott started to stand, and his hands were in the air.

"That does seem to be the subtext, doesn't it?" I mirrored his movement, putting my hands in the air, standing up. I left Zack at my feet, and Reed was lying on the ground next to where Scott stood.

They approached unspeaking, their guns trained on us. I spun around slowly, taking in all 360 degrees. We were well and truly surrounded, they had us covered from multiple approaches, and there was no escape in any direction. "You win, guys," Scott said. "So what is it? Prisoners or dead?"

The leader didn't respond, but his goggles were on his forehead and I could see his eyes. I didn't love the look of them. I could hear the faint hum of something, and I suspected it was an earpiece tuned a little too loud. My senses became heightened, the smell of the men around me pungent in my nose – Scott, Reed and Zack were each wearing some sort of cologne, gunpowder was heavy in the air, and the men in black had it on them along with something else, something more potent – gun oils, and blood.

It wasn't actually blood, but there was something in my head that was screaming, in the back, about blood. It was in their eyes, their posture, the way they moved. A faint voice was trying desperately to get out of a place I had locked him for a very long time.

Death, little doll, they mean you death...

They will kill you. I heard the voice of Aleksandr Gavrikov within. *They will snuff you out the way they were always trained, like the dogs of war they are...*

As amazing as it sounds, I saw Scott stiffen; he was looking at me and had noticed the change in my posture. "What?" he asked, sotto voce.

"The voices in my head say that they're going to kill us."

I saw the leader raise his submachine gun as if to answer me, and I could see his finger tightening on the trigger.

Chapter 4

Adrenaline raced through my veins, and the sound of the chopper blades overhead was deafening. I smelled the blood, even heavier now, and I realized it was on me, on my coat, and my shirt – Andromeda's blood. I wanted to hurt them, even as I watched their fingers tighten on their triggers; they were going so quick, there was no way I could stop them in time. And then I heard something else.

"GERONIMO!"

I was already moving before it registered that I recognized the voice. I heard and felt a rush of wind behind me and realized that two of the gunmen at my back had just been snugged to the ground by nets of light, something familiar to me from having experienced it in training. I leapt as I saw Scott shoot a jet of pressurized water out of his hands in two directions at once, sending two more of our enemies flying.

I heard the impact of a landing behind me, the sound of some dumbass – one Clyde Clary, in point of fact – shaking the earth with the weight of his bulk. I had a suspicion that ol' Clyde had transformed himself into either movable rock or metal before he hit the ground. He'd probably landed on one or two of those guys that had been pointing guns at us, judging by the wet splattering sound I heard as I flew through the air toward the leader of the squad.

I saw his eyes widen, but his gun began to adjust aim immediately and was already firing when I was just a foot away from him. I caught two rounds, but my momentum carried me through as I felt sharp pressure in my arm and shoulder from the impact of the bullets and in my head as I rammed it into his nose, breaking it.

I landed on my feet, woozy, but maintaining my balance. The man in black was not so lucky; I heard his head hit the ground and his body bounced at least twice before coming to rest about ten feet from me. The searing pain in my arm caught up to me and I sunk to my knees. It felt like someone was stabbing into my left bicep and shoulder, then twisting around in radial circles for kicks. I sank back, letting the pain overwhelm me.

Scott appeared at my side, the trees swaying above him, framing his head like some sort of bizarre nature picture. A blue-white sky provided the backdrop. "Damn, Sienna," he said, and his fingers came up with blood on the tips from where he touched my arm. "Not good."

"Took that bastard out, though," I said, trying not to make the kind of noise that would suggest I was hurt in any way. I blew my breath out through my lips and felt the tension in my guts as I bottled up the urge to scream. "Some of us don't have a ranged attack to deliver us from harm."

"Oh, yeah, harm," he said, sarcasm oozing out. "I was certainly never in any of that—"

"You two are bickering like kids." I heard a familiar voice as someone else stepped into Scott's lovely arboreal picture. Glen Parks, my instructor, appeared to Scott's left, his shaggy gray hair and beard such a contrast to his dark eyes. There was red in the beard around his mouth and he caught me looking. "Not mine," he said. "Got your sniper." We'd all been his pupils in training, Scott, Kat and I – but I always had this suspicion, based on the way he talked to me, that I was his favorite. Probably because I could fight better than either of them. Or it might just have been that our personalities meshed well – he had an edge about him, and I walked around like I was covered in barbed wire, daring anyone to get close to me.

"How's it look?" Scott asked, and his voice betrayed the tension.

"She's been shot," Parks said, as if to add, *you idiot.* "Twice. How do you think it looks?"

"Like a gunshot wound?" He paused. "Like two gunshot wounds?"

Parks didn't answer. I felt his fingers poke at one of my wounds and I let out the slightest moan without realizing I was the one making the sound. I saw other faces behind them – one of them was Clyde Clary's, his round face and blondish hair looking particularly long. I hadn't seen him for a few days, I realized, and I hadn't missed him. At all. "Clary," I said, acknowledging him with a little bit of a hiss in my voice.

"What's up, girl?" he asked, looking over the shoulders of Scott and Parks. "You wearing a tank top? Where's your gloves?" He looked at me blankly for a minute, nodding, his lips turning into a smile that I suspected was knowing – by which I mean it was knowing nothing. "Oh, I get it – you was throwing some hurt on people, giving 'em the ol' soul suck."

"Could you make that sound any dirtier?" Scott said, glaring at him over his shoulder.

"Sure," Clary said. "She was—"

"Shut up," Parks said, as another face appeared next to Clary's, this one looking at me from upside down. I almost didn't recognize it, because the long blond hair that had been there when I last saw her was gone, replaced with scorched skin that hadn't healed yet. One of her eyes was blank, sightless, but the other was still there and cold blue.

"Eve?" I asked, and the woman nodded. "What happened to you?"

"Battle scars," she said in her Germanic accent, "from my time in Kansas." She focused back on Parks. "The two I caught in my nets killed themselves with cyanide capsules in hollow teeth.

Same with the others." Her scarred face didn't show much, as though her nerves had been destroyed when she'd been burned.

"You're telling me we took them all out and have no prisoners to show for it?" Parks stopped what he was doing and looked up at her. "What about the chopper?"

"Flew off," she replied. "Roberto said they were headed southwest, but since we can't track them on radar…"

"They got away," Parks finished, and turned back to me. He took a small strip of fabric out of his beltpack and I felt him wrap it around my arm. "Dr. Perugini is gonna pull any bullets out that might be left inside you," he said to me. "My skills as a field surgeon are at their limit."

"Just do it," I said. "Get a pair of tweezers and do it. You know as well as I do that if you get them out now, I'll heal in the next few hours and be fine as a fiddle or whatever. You wait, and take me in that helicopter, and this flight is gonna suck for me."

Parks had a smile hidden beneath his blood-soaked beard. "Kid, this flight is gonna suck for you no matter what. But you got it." I heard the respect in the way he said it, and it meant something. At least for the five seconds it took for the agonizing pain to start. Clary turned metal and pushed me down, forcing my legs and arms into the dirt. I saw a flash of light, and I didn't know whether it was Eve using a net to bind me to the ground to keep me from squirming, the sun overhead going nova, or just the pain overwhelming my other senses.

I could still smell blood, mine and that of others, mingled with the dirt, the sweat, and the other smells of the world around me. The steady thrum of the chopper landing in the field next to us was muted, as were the urgent, insistent conversations being held by my comrades. I struggled when the pain got worse, trying not to. I focused on Kat first, thinking of her, of where she might be; then thought of my mother, who had kidnapped Kat for some unknown reason. Then I thought about Zack, and turned my head to see that Eve was tending to both him and Reed, who seemed to be starting to come around.

Lastly, my thoughts turned to Andromeda. I had known her for only hours, and she had already saved my life twice. I slammed my head against the forest floor, trying to resist the pain, both physical and mental, and I pushed my hair against the dirt and leaves, grinding my skull against it, into it, feeling the sharp pressure of some rocks and sticks poking at me. As the pain got worse, surging up my arm, my thoughts were reduced to a staccato burst.

Kat gone. Mom back, then gone again. Andromeda, dead. I was eighteen years old, and she wasn't the first person I had seen die, nor was she the first to die for me. Not even close. I pushed harder against the ground, and my right hand found a rock. I pushed it into my palm, felt the smooth contours, felt it give way and break under the pressure of my grip. I screamed, unintentionally. It felt like the stabbing pain was back, a million times worse, and when my eyes snapped open, the pretty blue-white background above was blood red. It suddenly felt far away, far, far away from me, the sky above just a pinprick of light that faded the smaller it got.

Chapter 5

I awoke hours later, in the medical unit at the Directorate. I remembered nothing of the chopper ride home, or of being wheeled in. The steady beeping of a monitor gave me the first clue of where I was as I opened my eyes. The second was the sight of a hospital bed next to mine, filled with the corpulent frame of Kurt Hannegan.

"Welcome back," he said, his weathered skin looking especially bad in the overhead fluorescent light. "Next time, wait until I'm discharged before you wake up, will you?" Petulant. Lovely.

"If I waited for you to discharge," I said, my throat feeling scratchy, "prematurely, and whatnot…connect the dots and make your own insult out of that, will you?" I waved my hand at him, the pulse-oxygen monitor hampering my ability to do it. I felt woozy and his face was distorted, as though someone were playing with a funhouse mirror in front of him.

"That the best you got?" He looked at me, unimpressed. The smooth metal walls of the medical unit and the hospital beds were running together.

"When it comes to you, Hannegan, do I really need any better?" I tried to shake off the wooziness, but I started to feel sick. "What the hell am I on?"

"Painkillers and chloridamide," I heard a voice say. I turned, and it felt like I was moving underwater. Dr. Perugini was there, walking toward me from her office. "I didn't want to give you both at the same time, but Scott said you were starting to hear the voices."

"I was," I said, "when we were in the woods. I hadn't taken

the chloridamide since…the night before last, I think."

She was at my side then, her white lab coat falling to below her knees, the dress she wore underneath it something of a blur. It was blue, I thought – no, yellow. My vision was changing color like the lights in a disco. Which I had never actually seen, except on TV. But that's what it looked like. "What color is your dress?" I asked her.

"It's black," she said, after staring at me pityingly for a moment. "You'll be fine in the morning, and I think we'll avoid giving you any more painkillers tonight."

"Probably for the best," I said. "Is Zack all right? And Reed? And—"

"Thanks for asking about me," Kurt said.

"Both fine." She waved her arm at the beds behind her. Zack was lying in the one nearest me, Reed in the one just past him. Neither appeared to be conscious. "Zack will need a few days to recover before he'll be fully healed, but your other friend is fine; just sedated and resting right now."

"Did they get Andromeda's body out of the woods?" I felt a tug of sorrow that I wished I didn't feel at all.

"Yes," Perugini answered. I let the question rest, the haze surrounding my mind not permitting me to think deeper about it. Perugini excused herself a moment later, returning to her office where I saw her through the blinds, making a phone call. She hung up and glanced back out at me, then sat at her desk and began working on something.

I spent the next few minutes trying not to talk to Kurt, who seemed equally eager not to talk to me. I was in no condition to trade barbs with him anyway, feeling heavy of tongue and slow of mind. I was fairly certain he'd say that that was normal.

The doors to the medical unit slid open a few minutes later with a gentle whoosh. Ariadne came in first, her usual gray suit with skirt combo not doing any wonders for her pale complexion.

Her red hair was light, and this time bundled over her shoulder in a ponytail, out of the way, an afterthought. I understood that, not liking to spend much time on my hair either, but I always thought she might be taking it to an extreme. She wore no makeup; or at least so little as to be unnoticeable, which meant her faded lips blended with her cheeks, and her eyelashes didn't stand out at all.

Old Man Winter followed her, his nearly seven-foot tall frame barely fitting through the door. He didn't even pretend to duck, and instead acted as though the top of the door frame would move out of the way for him. I couldn't be sure, as I was much closer to the ground and looking up, but I suspected he only missed bumping the top of his head by centimeters.

"Ariadne," I said as she approached. "You aren't in Kansas anymore." I looked down at her feet. "And no ruby slippers, though that's hardly a surprise."

"How are you feeling?" Ariadne said as she came to a stop by my bedside. "Are you competent to answer a few questions?"

"You maybe ought to ask the doctor about that," I said, "because I'm on a couple drugs at present, and they're making the whoosh go room."

She looked to Old Man Winter, as though seeking some form of confirmation from him. She did this frequently, but I rarely noticed him do anything that would indicate that he was responding to her. She turned back to me. "We need to know what happened."

"Pretty simple," I said. "We made good our escape from the Omega facility, and about an hour from home they took out our car with an RPG," I said. "You should consider equipping your cars with more weapons. If we'd had a few guns we might have made a better showing of it."

"It was a rental," Ariadne said. "Hannegan and Davis picked it up in Detroit and drove it all the way to their rendezvous with you."

"I bet the bill for that one Hertz," I said, clearly off-kilter if I was venturing into the land of puns.

Ariadne gave me an insincere smile. "Why don't you stick to the story at hand?"

"They ambushed us," I said, and felt a little emotion stir. "They ran us down, chased us through the woods, and they killed Andromeda. They had us surrounded, and they were about to kill us when M-Squad showed up and saved our bacon, our sausage, and every other fine pork product we possess."

Ariadne's arms were crossed, probably the most common posture the woman used. "Any indication for why they wouldn't have recaptured Andromeda instead of killing her?"

"They didn't give me any indications at all," I said. "The only reason I knew they were going to kill us was because my Greek chorus told me so; Wolfe and Gavrikov told me they were going to murder us instead of capture."

Old Man Winter showed a hint of movement at that. What would be regarded as nothing more than the twitch of a facial nerve in others was almost a full-blown look of horror on him. "Did Wolfe or Gavrikov give you any reason for this?"

"They didn't say anything after that. Probably got lost in the shuffle. Or possibly the screaming after I got shot." I frowned. "None of the enemy survived?"

"No," Ariadne said. "They all killed themselves."

"I remember hearing that. Cyanide? Who does that?" I shook my head.

"Apparently Omega," Ariadne said. "I can't say I've met a lot of fanatics willing to kill themselves rather than be caught."

"That's a shame," I said without any remorse at all. "We've got bigger problems, though."

"Agreed," Ariadne said. "This war between us and Omega – scratch that, this war that Omega has completely blindsided us with – is disastrous. We finally score a single victory and it's snatched out of our hands hours later."

"I'm sure Andromeda would feel poorly about the fact that you're losing this war that she knew nothing about," I said icily, "you know, if she hadn't just gotten killed while not even being a part of it. But by bigger problem, I meant something else." I clenched my jaw. "She said something just before she died – that we had a traitor in the Directorate."

"Are you kidding?" Ariadne asked, her calm demeanor unraveling slightly. She blinked several times in rapid succession, shook her head, then looked to Old Man Winter, who stood still as ever. "How...who?"

"She didn't say," I replied. "But she had some strange abilities, and one of them was to...I don't know, see beyond...somehow. She knew things she shouldn't have known, and it wouldn't surprise me if she figured this one out. It was almost like she knew she was going to die before it happened."

"Did she tell you anything else?" Old Man Winter asked. "Anything at all?"

"She told us quite a bit – and we learned quite a bit about Omega even before this," I said wryly. "Would you like to know who Omega is?" I saw Ariadne lean forward, curiosity consuming her. Old Man Winter was as implacable as ever as I stared back at him. "Or do you already know?"

"I know," he said, his words thickly accented. "I knew them when they ran the old world, when the sun did not rise or set without sacrifices being made in their names. I knew them when the influence they exerted over the world of men began to diminish. I knew them when they began putting themselves atop governments and parliaments, passing for humans while working the levers of power to their own benefit. I have seen them in the palaces of the old world and the penthouses of the new, and I know every one of their names, living and dead, because I knew them before their rise and after their fall."

"I'm sorry, what?" Ariadne asked, looking at her boss with

barely disguised incredulity. "Who is Omega?"

"They're the old gods," I said, smirking, causing Ariadne to whipsaw back around to me. "The Greek ones, the Asian, Arabic, Norwegian and so on – the ones that ruled the world in ancient times, in myth and legend. It sounds like they miss the good old days." I kept focused on Old Man Winter, who nodded subtly. "So do you know what they're after?"

"Hard to say," he replied, back to unexpressive. "The natural instinct would be to suggest they would like a return to the world of old, the one they ruled. Such a thing seems improbable, though, given the proliferation of technologies that both make their lives easier and also allow humans to kill them with a simplicity that was not to be found in the days when they held dominion over the affairs of men. They faded to the background for good reason, you know."

"So you don't know what they want, either," I said, mildly disappointed, "other than money and power."

"All men want money and power," Old Man Winter said. "The only difference is scale of ambition and the means they are willing to use to acquire them."

"Well that sounds fun," Ariadne said, interjecting herself back into the conversation. "But if they're the old gods, why are they attacking us? What does killing our agents and metas get them?"

"Access to money or power, I'd guess." I said it, but Old Man Winter nodded along with me. "They're playing a long game, especially if they've been alive for thousands of years. The moves they're making don't seem to make any sense by the reasonable standards I'd set, but they're doing something – they're after something – to make their objective reachable. The problem is we don't know their objective, and so their means are completely incomprehensible." I shrugged. "Like an episode of Lost."

"Cute," Ariadne said. "But that doesn't put us any closer to why they wrecked western Kansas trying to kill off our strongest metas, or why they triggered a major operation that killed dozens of our agents." She paused in thought, face pensive. "What kind of powers did Andromeda exhibit? The ability to…read minds?"

"Not minds," I said. "Not quite. More like the ability to see things that were going to happen, to know things about people and events. She said she knew everything about Omega and was going to tell us. Then she seemed to know she was going to die. But another time, it was like she could see through a wall and knew what kind of car Zack and Kurt were driving."

"That was freaky," Hannegan said from behind me. "But it might not have been her seeing through walls. If she was a telepath, she could have read our minds to know what we were driving."

"Not a bad point," Ariadne said with a nod of the head after I failed to answer. "Any other powers?"

"She could touch my skin without being drained," I said. "And when she did touch me, it was like my pain subsided. What kind of a meta can do all that?" I looked to Old Man Winter.

He cleared his throat, and slowly, ponderously slowly, began to answer. "Only one kind can touch an incubus or succubus without being drained – but I assure you she was not one of…those." There was a glassiness in his gaze as he said it. "She could be some hybrid of powers given her by her parents, as has been known to occur from time to time – something new."

"Would Dr. Sessions know?" I asked.

"Unlikely," Old Man Winter said. "His study is limited to the things he can quantify."

Something broke loose in my mind as I put together something Perugini said earlier with Old Man Winter's words. "You're having him perform an autopsy…experiments…on Andromeda." I said it sadly, stifling the sense of outrage I felt over the violation of her body.

"An autopsy." Ariadne gave me a pat on the shoulder. "No

real experiments, just…taking tissue samples, very close to what a coroner would do anyway."

"I see." The only reason I didn't lash out at them about it is because I could see the canniness in it, and in Ariadne's response. It caused me to burn a little, under the skin, metaphorically, but that was because I disliked the idea of her being…meddled with, as though it would affect her peace in death. For all I knew, she wasn't at all peaceful in death.

And even sadder for her…I realized at that moment that I was probably the only one in the entire world who actually cared that she was dead.

"What's the next move?" I tried to guide my brain onto a new track, away from that grim thought, before it favored me with the inevitable comparison between me and Andromeda – because I'd been where she was, without anyone to care whether I lived or died.

"We're at war," Ariadne said. "We have all our agents on re-call, every single campus is at a heightened state of alert. All six Directorate campuses have reported similar incidents, with human agents being drawn out on missions and slaughtered. We've lost something like seventy-five percent of our human resources in the course of the last few days, along with a few metas."

I started to ask something, to mention my amazement at the scope of that number and what it meant, but stopped when the doors slid open behind Old Man Winter and someone walked into the medical unit. I could feel the drugs affecting my system, be-cause I actually smiled when I saw who it was. I might have smiled anyway, if I knew no one else was around, but in this case I did it in spite of that. "What's up, Doc?"

"Been watching those Looney Tunes DVDs I lent you?" The wide smile that greeted me in return was good enough to give me a warm, fuzzy feeling. Dr. Quinton Zollers made his way across the medical unit to my other bedside, after greeting Ariadne and

Old Man Winter with a perfunctory nod. "I had a feeling you'd have an appreciation for Wile E. Coyote, after all you've been through." He looked down at me, and his mocha skin crinkled around the eyes. "Maybe even more, now."

"Yeah, I don't remember the bullets in those cartoons doing quite this kind of damage," I said, pointing toward my afflicted arm. "I expected some general scorching all about my body, but this? Ouch."

"Thought I'd check on you," Zollers said. "Heard you ran into your mom."

"I did," I said. "And as much as I'd loooove to talk about it…" I wouldn't, but I'd be willing to with Zollers more than anyone else. "…we were just discussing the war."

Zollers frowned, his dark face made darker still by his expression. "We've lost a lot of good people in the last few days."

"More to come if we're not careful," Ariadne said. "And if it's really true we have a traitor in our midst—"

"Traitor?" Zollers asked, scrunching his face. "Where'd this come from?"

"Andromeda," I said, and met his gaze; I could see the concern in him. "She told me before she got killed by those Omega gunmen."

"I see," Zollers said. "Well, that's a kink in our garden hose."

"To put it mildly," Old Man Winter said. "If true, I want this traitor ferreted out."

"How do you propose to do that?" Ariadne said. "I mean, we have a staff of hundreds just at this campus, assuming here was where Andromeda meant, and assuming she knew what she was talking about."

"You can narrow that down," I said. "These guys, this attack, it wasn't random. We were on US Highway 8, taking the long way home to try and avoid getting hit – you can't tell me they sent a helicopter along every major route to the cities. Someone knew where we were, knew we were coming, and it's because they either managed to figure out how to trace our cell phones or because someone gave them our route."

Ariadne exchanged a look with Old Man Winter. "Only a dozen, maybe a few more knew that you were on your way back. But there aren't that many likely routes back to the Directorate. Interstate 94 may be the most likely, but Highway 8 is not that far out of the question. They may have scanned 94 and then gone to the alternate as soon as they realized you weren't there."

"I don't think so," I said. "The timing is all wrong. They hit us at an isolated point in the road, one of the last few. They hit us with an RPG, which required some effort to set up the shot, and—"

"They caught us at the worst possible moment," Kurt said, interrupting and drawing the attention back to him. "There's no way they caught us by pure accident. They knew. They knew we were on that road, at that time."

"They could have traced our cellphones, though," I said. "It wouldn't be the first time it's happened even on this trip."

"Did you have your cellphone on you?" Kurt looked at me, expectant.

"No; it got destroyed...in the last car that blew up when they fired a rocket at it," I said sheepishly.

"Remind me not to go for a Sunday drive with you," Zollers said.

"So, I didn't have mine," I said. "The question is, did Scott have his? Did Zack?"

"Zack did," Ariadne said. "It's how we tracked you down to send in M-Squad. He had the line open to us."

"And I had him," I said. "Good thing we didn't leave him behind."

"Yeah," Kurt said, dark clouds brewing upon his face, "unlike some poor bastards I know."

"They kept on us when we were out there, too," I pointed out. "They followed us relentlessly. Scott and I assumed they had a thermal imaging device of some sort, tracking our body heat, but they may have just been tracking Zack's cell phone."

"That's not easy to do," Ariadne said. "It'd take a hell of an expert to track the GPS in a phone. And you'd have to know what phone you're looking for, first."

"Which is where your traitor would come in," Zollers said. "If they knew who was on the mission, they could pass along the cell number and allow Omega to track them down. Further, this is hardly the sort of deeply traitorous stuff that you'd expect. It could have been done by someone unintentionally."

"How do you inadvertently give away the cell phone numbers of agents in a manner that gets them killed?" Kurt asked.

"Simple enough," Zollers said. "My work cell phone, for instance, contains the numbers for almost every agent in the Directorate's Minneapolis campus. All it would take is for my cell phone to be viewed by another party for them to have all the numbers for every single person who's been hunted and killed in the last few days. The person whose phone was viewed wouldn't even necessarily have to know about it – perhaps they simply..." He hesitated. "...were deceived. They might have...slept with someone, stepped into the shower and allowed them access to their cell phone..."

I felt scarlet creep up my cheeks, hot embarrassment at Zollers' words, at the suggestion. All it took to get people killed was the numbers of every agent they wanted tracked down, pilfered from a Directorate Operative's cell phone by someone from Omega, unsupervised. Someone like James Fries.

"We could search through everyone," Ariadne said, "for months, and still come up dry. This is...so much data. So many people. How do you even start?"

"You don't need to start," I said, feeling the dark cloud settling in over me. "It was me. I left my cell phone in my hotel room last night with an Omega operative," I said, "while I was on the conference call with you, Ariadne. I didn't know he was Omega at the time, and I didn't know what would happen, but it was me…I left it in there with him for at least a half-hour." I shook my head, and pummeled myself inside for my supreme stupidity. "It was me."

Chapter 6

The room seemed to freeze around me, the life drained out of it like air all exhaled in one great breath. I didn't want to look up at any of them, but when I did, I saw Ariadne staring at me in numbest shock, her mouth open and trying to move, caught comically agape. Zollers cleared his throat and looked away, which was, I think, the worst reaction of them all. I heard Kurt snort on the bed behind Zollers, but I didn't much care about him.

"What..." Ariadne stumbled over her attempt to speak, then recovered, her face going through several changes of expression. "What were you..." Her eyes rolled back, like she was trying to recall something, and I saw her white-knuckle the railing of my bed, before she finally managed a full sentence. "What...was he doing there?"

"Waiting for me," I said. I caught a hint of disappointment from Zollers, though he hid it well. "He was an incubus, and so he could – we could—"

"I don't need to hear any more," Ariadne said, waving a hand in front of me to cut me off. "I'm going to send our staff investigator to debrief you. He's going to start putting together a picture of what you know about Omega, and how this happened."

"If I may," Old Man Winter said, in a tone that let us know he wasn't so much asking for permission to interject as he was warning everyone else to shut up. "While this...Omega operative may have gotten access to your cell phone, it was not the cause of our recent setbacks. The ambush of our agents was in motion prior to your call with Ariadne, and the battle in Kansas was already underway." He looked at me, boring into my eyes. "You are not responsible for this. The fault rests with someone else."

Ariadne seemed to think about this for a moment. "Very well. They couldn't have gotten the data from her phone. I still want our investigator to talk to you about this – this – this—" She stopped, closed her eyes, and exhaled. "All right." She shook her head again. "Anything else, tell the investigator. His name is Michael Mormont." She shook her head and turned to leave.

Old Man Winter waited, still staring me down, but after another moment he broke off and followed her. He stopped at the door and turned. "You saw your mother."

"I did," I said, afraid to meet his eyes. Why did I feel this overwhelming sense of shame? Probably because I got suckered by an Omega operative who damned near got me to lose my virginity to him less than twenty-four hours before he beat the hell out of me.

"Did she say anything?" he asked. "Anything of consequence?" His hand was on the door, on the metal frame around it, and I saw a small sheen of ice spreading out on the steel in a light spiderweb pattern, radiating out from his hand across the metal wall.

"No," I said. "Just told me I'd screwed up and that I'd screw up again." I clenched my fist and felt pain shoot through my arm where I'd been shot. "Just like always," I whispered.

Old Man Winter nodded. "She has always been…a hard woman. My chosen surname is Winter," he said, with the slightest smile, "but she is the very definition of it – harsh, unrelenting, unforgiving."

"You used to work with her at the Agency?" I asked, referring to the government-controlled precursor to the Directorate. No one had ever really explained to me what happened to the Agency, other than that it was destroyed.

"Our paths would cross occasionally. She was an agent, one of the best. I was in…administration. I knew her only in passing."

"What happened?" I asked, in genuine wonder. "What happened when the Agency was destroyed? Why did she flee, give up her name and everything and hide for almost two decades?"

"Fear, I would think," Old Man Winter said, possibly breaking some kind of personal record for number of consecutive sentences in a row. "Fear for you and your safety. It is a dangerous world for metas." His eyes narrowed. "And especially for a succubus."

I opened my mouth to ask another question about the Agency and its destruction, but as though he sensed he didn't want to answer it, he left, the doors sliding shut behind him. "What was that supposed to mean?" I asked Zollers, who chewed his lip as he watched Old Man Winter leave.

"I don't know. Not being a meta myself, I suppose I'm not down with the lingo."

"'Down with the lingo'?" I asked. "Did you really just talk like a geek fanboy?"

"Naw," he said, "that was totally street." He paused, tried to keep a straight face, and then smiled. "The street where the comic shop is located, anyway. So…" he said, "I need to talk to you."

"Why?" I asked, distracted, staring at the doors that Old Man Winter had just walked out of. "Did I do something wrong?" I asked mockingly.

"Sounds like," Zollers replied, "but that's not why I want to talk to you. Standard Directorate procedure after you've been through a firefight. Gotta make sure you're not suffering from Post Traumatic Stress Disorder."

"I'm suffering from multiple gunshot wounds," I said. "I'm suffering from a lack of answers and an abundance of questions—"

"Something I'm sure you've never dealt with ever, at any point in your life."

I let that hang in the air for a second, then blew air out of my lips and shook my head, only mildly amused. "You know me too well, Doctor."

"I try," he said. "You could make it easier, though. Come see me when you get out. And you know." He looked at me with a narrowed, piercing gaze that was coupled with a knowing smile to devastating effect. "If you don't, I will hunt you down."

"I've been made aware of that before, yes."

"All right, then," he said with a nod, then hesitated, as though he remembered or realized something. He looked at me somewhat tenderly, then nodded again and walked out, his posture stiff. I started to ask him what that was about, but shrugged. We all act a little weird sometimes.

As the doors shut, I heard movement to my left and turned to look. Reed was still asleep in the corner of the medical unit closest to Dr. Perugini's office, but there was motion in the bed next to him.

It was Zack. His eyes were open and fixed on me, and his face was crumpled in a way that caused my heart to drop in my chest. His lips were twisted, eyes squinting, emotion plastered over every inch of his handsome face, and I had another jolt of realization – he had been listening when I told the others about James, about what I had done.

"I'm sorry," I said. He didn't reply. He just shook his head, bowing it down. After a moment he looked back at me in silent accusation, then closed his eyes and rolled over, giving me nothing but a view of his back.

Chapter 7

I got discharged from the medical unit a few hours later. Zack still wouldn't speak to me, and I didn't bother trying very hard because truthfully, I was more than a little ashamed. I mean, I was nearly in bed with another guy less than twenty-four hours after breaking up with Zack. Not my best day ever.

I stepped out of the headquarters building to find the sun shining, fluffy white clouds draped intermittently across the sky, with a warm wind pushing them along. It was a beautiful summer's day and not too hot, for once. The scent of fresh cut grass permeated the air in front of headquarters.

Dr. Perugini had had someone retrieve clothes from my room, so I was walking out of the medical unit in a pair of jeans and a loose fitting long-sleeved T-shirt. My arm still felt a little painful, but the place where the bullets had been pulled out only the day before were now simply angry red spots, just a little scabbing giving any indication that there was ever any deeper injury there.

I didn't want to think about the internal pressure I had weighing on me – not about Mom, nor Zack, nor James, not about Omega, or anything, really. I knew Ariadne's investigator, Michael Mormont, would find me sooner or later, and I was sure that would be a joyous exploration of my many screw-ups, but I counted myself lucky that I'd been unconscious when he'd stopped by the medical unit earlier.

No, I needed a distraction right now. I didn't have an assignment, and I was done with training—

I stopped walking. Parks had hammered it into our heads, over and over, that we were never done with training. "Training never ends," Parks had said, his dark eyes visible beneath his gray, bushy eyebrows. "Not for the true professional. Training's a way of life for the prepared, for people who are always looking for the edge in a fight. And you never know when that fight will come."

I understood him in a way that Kat and Scott had never quite come around to. It made sense to me. Probably because my mom had the same philosophy, and we had trained every day, on martial arts, on weapons, on fighting.

I found my feet carrying me past the newly rebuilt science labs, past the gym, to a nondescript building tucked at the far side of the sprawling Directorate campus. The gym housed workout equipment, suitable for employees to exercise and maintain physical fitness. But this was the training center, a three-story boxy building of concrete and metal. It housed a gun range, a full martial arts studio, and a dozen classrooms with materials suitable for any lesson you wanted to learn.

I walked through the double glass doors and into the gray-carpeted hallway. The carpeting was thin, like it was just barely stretched over the concrete floor. I entered a drab hall that was all glass windows on both sides. I looked through the windows, which were bulletproof glass, down onto the firing range below. The stalls where the shooters stood were all empty, the range quiet.

I pushed open the heavy door that separated me from the range. All was quiet; I walked down the staircase, my tennis shoes squeaking against the rubber-plastic substance coating each stair. When I reached the bottom, the smell of gunpowder greeted me, the sweet smell of fired bullets. To my right was the rangemaster's armory, and I pulled open the door and walked in, drawing a raised eyebrow from the man behind the counter.

"I didn't expect to see you here," Glen Parks said, his lips puckered, giving his rugged face a skeptical tilt. "Being newly discharged from the medical unit, I assumed you'd have other things to do."

"I didn't enjoy being shot," I said, "and maybe some practice will help keep it from happening again."

"Not losing your gun next time would probably help more than target practice."

"I didn't just lose one, I lost two. And a backup knife."

It was hard to suss out his reaction, his face remaining mask-like even as his fingers drummed out a steady rhythm on the counter in front of him. "Good girl. You'll be needing some new ones, then?"

"I'd like to stick with my Sig and my Walther," I said, sidling up to the counter and leaning on it with my uninjured arm. "And I'd like to get some practice in; a couple hundred rounds with the Sig at least."

"And the Walther?" he asked.

"Fifty or so," I said, and he pulled boxes of bullets off the back shelves and set them on the counter, then walked to a cabinet behind him and opened it, rummaged around for a minute before coming back with two gun cases. He opened the first to reveal a Walther, then the second to reveal a Sig Sauer that was exactly like the one I had lost.

I took both pistols, their cases, and the bullets, along with the ear protection and eye protection, and went out onto the range. There was something therapeutic about having the gun in my hand. I pulled targets out of the bin in the corner; they were all black and white outlines of a vaguely man-shaped person. I hung the first from the clips and sent the target downrange with the little button that caused the hanger to zip along the cord. The paper target waved, fluttering along until it was a good fifteen feet away from me.

I put in ear plugs, then slipped the muffs over my ears. Having been exposed to a small war's worth of gunfire and explosions over the prior few days, I wondered if this would make any difference. I put on the eyewear, then pulled the Sig out of the sleeve. I smelled the unique hint of gun oil as I brought the slide up to my nose and took a deep sniff. I know it sounds weird, but I've always thought that after a while, the faded smell of gun oil smells just a little like curry.

I fired through a hundred rounds pretty quickly, stopping a few times between magazines to change the target. I looked at my results every time I reeled in the silhouette outlines. I visualized James Fries as the outline in the targets and it seemed to help. There could be no doubt I needed more practice with a gun. Even though I felt fairly confident I could put a severe hurting on someone, my mother would have viewed anything less than flawless results as an indicator that we needed to practice more. Flawless results only meant you needed to maintain your skills in this area, and focus on becoming better somewhere else.

The next hundred bullets went smoother, and I felt the kink in my shoulder dissolving. Whatever scar tissue was left from my encounter with the Omega gunman was disappearing thanks to my meta healing. I thought about Zack, still lying in the medical unit, unable to heal anywhere nearly as quickly as me.

I missed the next shot completely, didn't even hit the target.

He was weaker than I was, no doubt. His human physiology made him more prone to injury and less likely to shake it off. I'd had occasions where I'd been beaten nearly to death and twenty-four hours later there wasn't a sign I'd even been hit. He, on the other hand, scarred. He bled, heavily, and for longer. I wasn't sure if I was even still thinking about his injury. Now I was thinking about the look on his face when he found out about James.

I missed two more shots in a row, and didn't bother for a third. I set the gun on the counter in front of me and took a deep breath.

I was reeling in the target when I heard gunfire from the stall next to me. Absorbed in my own problems, I hadn't even noticed someone else enter the range, which was sloppy on my part. For the girl who always seems to have an Omega operative chasing her, paying zero attention is the fastest way to an ugly end. I stepped back from my spot, my booth, I thought of them, even though there was just a divider between me and the next positions on either side – and looked left. Someone ran through an entire magazine, fast, fifteen shots in rapid succession. I looked down-range and saw their target; it was fresh, and holes were appearing in it, most outside the silhouette of the human body at the center. In gun terms, that's what we like to call 'whoops'. That might not just be in gun terms, actually.

I caught a glimpse of curly, sandy blond hair as the shooter stepped back for a minute, rolling his shoulders as though trying to work some tension out of them. I didn't want to offer unsolicited advice, but it wasn't going to do a thing to improve his accuracy if he didn't slow down and stop trying to blast through all fifteen rounds in ten seconds. I might have said it, too, but I knew better in this case. Hiding behind the clear plastic glasses that were sup-posed to protect him from stray shell casings was the face of Scott Byerly – solemn, determined and serious.

I approached Scott slowly from behind, taking my time as he ran through another magazine, managing to land only his first couple shots inside the silhouette. The most he could have hoped for was that the proximity of his fire would cause the perpetrator to suffer from a fearful case of soiled pants, because the bullets were unlikely to stop him unless he somehow leapt in front of one of them in a panic.

When he was finished, Scott stepped back and laid his gun down on the counter in front of him, barrel pointed downrange. If he'd known much about how to use a firearm, or if he'd been pay-ing more attention during Parks' lessons, he probably would have treated it more gingerly. He didn't, though, and his face was stormy as I approached. He heard me, I knew, because his shoul-ders slumped as I came up behind him.

"Hey," I said, pulling my ear protection down to rest around my neck. I pulled the ear plugs out and put them in my pocket, the little pliant pieces of foam only slightly larger than the first knuckle of my pinky finger. "How are you holding up?"

He didn't answer, but stepped back to the gun, slapped another magazine into it and ran through the whole thing in about ten seconds, one shot after another. I barely had time to get my earmuffs back on before he loosed it, and when he was done, he still gave no indication that he'd seen or heard me. Of course, I knew he had. He was tense, his posture unnatural, stiffer than the usually laid-back Scott. He never took anything seriously. Or almost anything, I thought, remembering back to the time we'd met and clashed because I'd been responsible for the deaths of friends of his, then members of his family.

I sat there as he fiddled with the gun, reloading a magazine from a box of 9mm bullets sitting next to him. I waited, wanting to see if he'd even acknowledge me, wondering if for some reason he blamed me for something I had nothing to do with. After a moment, I turned and started away, my earmuffs back around my neck, hugging the sides of it snug.

"You think she fought?" Scott asked. I turned, and saw he was still loading the magazine, pushing the bullets into the clip with fumbling fingers. One dropped and it pinged against the concrete floor. He stooped to pick it up. "You think your mom hit her? Knocked her out? Or do you think Kat just went along with her?"

I had to think about it. What we'd seen of the car my mom had been driving gave some clues. The interior was bloody, and there was a bullet hole in the car's upholstery. The fact that she'd used her hands to drain the memories of our agents that had been riding with Kat was a sign that she had probably done the same with Scott's girlfriend. "I think my mom took her," I said, stating an opinion I could only back up through conjecture, "because she realized she was a Persephone-type, and that…tends to be useful."

"Yeah, I get that," he said, almost snarling, and jammed another bullet into the magazine with savagery, pushing hard against the spring as if he could throttle it into giving Kat back to him. "What I'm asking you is if Kat just went along or if she fought your mom."

"I think she fought," I said, answering without thinking about it. I knew what he wanted to hear, and I sensed that anything else I said could be dangerous. Not for me, because I had all the confidence in the world that I could flatten him before he could so much as raise the gun at me (not that he would), but for him and his fragile state of mind. "Kat's not the sort of girl that would let a stranger abduct her without putting up a fight." After a second of reflection, I realized that this was probably true; no lie needed, even though I apparently was prepared to deliver one without thinking about it. Kat was a fighter; not, perhaps, as much as I would have considered myself to be one, but she was no weakling. She may have been blessed with the power to heal, but I'd seen her put a hurting on a few people since we'd begun working together.

"Yeah, I think so too." Scott's shoulders slumped again, and the next bullet he tried to put into the magazine went easier. "Where do you think she took her? Your mom, I mean—"

"I don't know. I mean, we're talking about a woman who locked me in a box one day and disappeared, not to return for six months." I felt a tightness in my chest, a burning near my eyes, and I hated myself for it. "She's not exactly predictable, you know? I mean, I kinda thought she was dead until she showed up and kicked my Aunt Charlie's ass."

"You thought she was dead?" He turned away again. "And that didn't bother you?" His head tilted sideways to look at me.

I felt irritation rising, but was detached enough to realize it had little to do with Scott. "See above, re: locking me in a box and disappearing without warning or a trace. Not exactly behavior designed to build a warm and fluffy relationship with your offspring. She left me, Scott. To die, or to manifest and break out; either way, she left me to be picked off by Wolfe, and lucky for me the Directorate came along or who knows what Omega would be doing to me right now—"

"Huh." He picked up another silhouette target and hung it, his fingers exercising more care with the clips that held it in place than they had with loading the bullets. "If she just…left you to Wolfe and you're her daughter, what do you think she's doing to Kat right now?" He held the switch and the motor buzzed, sending the hangar zipping downrange, the target fluttering along with it. "Kat doesn't have anybody else," he said, and his eyes came up, and I caught the hint of violence within, the stir beneath the surface, threatening to boil out. "No one else to care if she were to disappear. Or die."

He turned, pointing the gun downrange, and I slapped my muffs back on as he began to fire. I heard every shot, each one a declaration of intent, the target a silent, black and white stand-in for my mother, each blast of primer and powder a small explosion of his rage blooming forth from the barrel of the gun. I turned my face away, as though I couldn't handle the spectacle of him shooting at the target that was my mother by proxy.

I could hear the click after the last of the bullets was spent, and I looked up at the target, still whole, not a single perforation in the silhouette. He stood there, unblinking, a sort of disbelief visible behind the clear plastic of his protective eyewear. He stared, his mouth slightly open for a moment before I saw the physical reaction break down his cold resolve. "Son of a…" he said, and I had to stifle the deep desire to laugh. "Dammit," he said, the timbre of his voice rising, and he threw the gun downrange where it clipped the bottom of the target, ripping it on the corner with the force of the throw. The gun continued, his meta strength carrying it all the way to the wall.

His hand came up again, and he extended a single finger. The air rippled around him, and a blast of water came out, focused, small, the size of a roll of pennies, and shot downrange. It impacted in the center of the target's blank-white face, ripping a hole through the middle of it as though one of his bullets had hit the target. The splash of the water against the concrete wall in the distance was audible. His other hand came up and a broader blast of water followed, one that tore the target from the hangar and left it a sopping mess on the floor.

Scott turned back to me, his face twisted, breathing heavy, as though he had exerted everything. Without saying anything else, he walked to the stairs and left. I looked back to the range, where a thin trail of water stretched from the counter to the where the destroyed target lay and threaded off into the distance behind it.

Chapter 8

I left the range shortly thereafter, leaving Parks with nothing but a friendly nod and a wave. I crossed the hall to the training room, an open space with a wall holding every imaginable kind of weapon, from the eskrima sticks that had brought me so much joy over the years, to sickles, scythes, bo staffs, and a full range of swords. There were a half-dozen excellent katanas, and I chose one that I had practiced with before, and began a kata – a series of regimented martial arts moves rendered in sequence – that utilized the sword.

I was graceful, I was elegant, I was lethal. I watched myself in the long wall of mirrors opposite the door and the glass windows that allowed people walking down the hallway to look in and see what I was doing. I suppose I would have cared if the building got more traffic. M-Squad would pop in and out infrequently, maybe once a week, doing their own thing, but most of the time they stuck to their own floor in the dorms, which was on the other side of the campus. Except Parks. He was here constantly. A way of life.

Otherwise, it was Scott, Kat and myself. Sometimes agents or other Directorate employees would come to the gun range to practice their firearms skills. I think the agents had to do a certain amount of practice per week as a part of their jobs, because I always tended to see them on the range on Monday morning. After that, it was pretty quiet.

Though after the last week, and the slaughter of so many of those agents by Omega, I guessed it was going to be quiet around here for a while, until they restaffed. If they restaffed.

I went through a kata I had done about a million and a half times before. Mom taught me dozens of them, in the basement, and most of them were interchangeable in terms of the weapon you could use – or no weapon at all. The katana was light and well-balanced enough for me to use it one-handed. I still struck with my other hand as a fist, practicing as if to pretend my primary hand, the one without the sword, were striking to stun, to distract, and then the blade followed up. You didn't use a blade unless you were ready to kill. Although you could wound with one, it was uncertain, and better not to take a chance with anything you didn't want dead. Mom taught me that. A blade raised in anger is for killing, nothing else.

I moved gracefully through the kata to the end and stopped, the blade poised. I stood there, sword at full extension, holding my position, and looked to the mirror to check my technique, which was flawless. It should be. I'd practiced it twenty times a week since I was twelve, with and without weapons. Even now, outside of my mother's influence, I found it to be the habit I couldn't break, the remnant of the past that kept coming back, even though she had disappeared. It stayed with me, and after Scott, Kat and Parks had all called it a day, I kept coming back here, to this place, and practicing, as though it were something that was so ingrained that it was in my core and couldn't be shed, like a second skin hiding beneath my first.

"Very nice," came the voice from the door. I hadn't heard it open, which was unusual, but then the man standing there with his arms folded was the disarming sort anyway, the type that I wouldn't have felt threatened by even if I'd seen him coming. He'd earned enough of my trust that I wouldn't have jumped like a scared cat; anyone else catching me in the middle of a form unexpectedly might have (would have) gotten a much different reaction.

"I didn't hear you come in," I said, and wiped my forehead,

my long sleeve catching the sweat that had begun to bead there. The practice room was actually quite comfortable, but my practice was exerting – every strike, block and attack was practiced at full tilt, nothing held back, but with all discipline and control. When I strung several katas together in sequence it became very good exercise, if I didn't take a break in between. I looked at the clock hanging over the door and realized I had been practicing for over an hour. "And it's not that easy to sneak up on me, so my congratulations."

"I don't think I can claim much credit for that," Dr. Zollers said, the irony bleeding through into his words. "The building could have been burning down around you and I doubt you would have noticed."

"Those are the things I tend to perceive," I said, finding my way back to the far wall and replacing the katana on the pegs that waited for it. The curved blade fitted perfectly into the scabbard and I hung it back where it belonged after wiping the sweat off the handle. "You know, black smoke billowing around the ceiling, heat spiking to uncomfortable levels, flames all around." I turned to find him unmoved, still standing by the door, relaxed. "Unthreatening psychiatrists in sweater vests don't tend to set off my smoke detectors."

"Ah," he said with a subtle nod. "Next time I'll set the room ablaze to get your attention. Or would that be too subtle?"

"There's not too much subtlety to burning down a room, no," I said, and wiped my face again. I craved water now that I had stopped moving. The dryness in my mouth caused my lips to smack together as though they were chapped. The cool air of the AC had also started to chill me now that I was done, the sheen of sweat around my skin getting cold as the air conditioner fought against the hot summer temperatures outside. "There's probably an easier way to get my attention if you're after it."

"Something like saying, 'Come to my office the minute you

get out of the medical unit'? Something gentle, but that communicates the urgency of the situation – which is that you, young lady, are required by your employers to go through post-stress debriefing to talk through your recent mission." He shook his head, almost like a tic, and went on. "Something that conveys that there's worry about the fact that you got pummeled, shot, beaten, lost a teammate, watched a girl die, and had an Omega lackey pull a fast one on you." His features tightened. "Maybe I really should have lit the room on fire, because that stuff all sounds kind of dire and in need of being discussed."

"It will be discussed," I said, biting my lower lip. "You heard Ariadne. It'll be discussed, sifted, pulled apart, probed – you get the picture," I said, restraining emotion again. "I'll be talking about it with their investigator."

"Sure," he said, halting a few steps away from me. If it had been anyone else, I might have flinched internally at their approach. I wouldn't show weakness by doing it physically, but it'd be there in my reaction. "You'll discuss the cold, dry details of the whole thing, over and over," he said, "poring over all the insignificancies you've probably forgotten, all the questions asked that need to be answered – all that," he said. "But you know what you won't talk about? How you feel."

"Feelings?" I asked with the hint of a smile. "I think you might be talking to the wrong girl. After all, I know they have some uncharitable names for me out there," I said, waving my hand in the direction of the outside, Directorate world. "Most don't think I have any of those."

"Who?" he asked, serious. "Who do you think talks about you that way?"

"The agents," I said. "The ones still alive, anyways. The metas, the ones who aren't in training. The rank and file. The administrators at HQ." I shrugged. "Eve Kappler. Everybody, just about."

"You think so?" He didn't deny it. "Got a persecution complex?"

"No," I said. "Just good hearing. I'm sure it'll be worse now."

Zollers frowned. "Why now?"

"Because it was my mom," I said, wearing a plastered, Cheshire cat-like smile. "Kat was like…the popular cheerleader on campus. Everybody liked her. My mother kidnapped her, and the rumor mill will go wild with speculation that I was involved, or that somehow it's my fault—"

"You may be leaping a bit far, there," he said. "The news that Kat's been taken by your mother hasn't even spread yet. And the people that do know – Ariadne, Director Winter, Scott – none of them believe that you're involved in any way."

"Oh?" I asked, still wearing that stupid smile. "How do you know for sure?"

He gave me a look, something between deep thought and rolling his eyes. "I just know. I'm supposed to not only know the people of the Directorate through little chat sessions like we're having here," he flicked his finger to point at me, then him, "but to get a pulse for the morale of the whole organization. So I've got the pulse, and here's where it is: those who know Kat's gone are worried about her. They don't think you were involved in your mom's plans in any way. Hasn't crossed their minds."

"And the rumors?" I asked, blood still cold. "Because when they find out the 'who' of it, they're going to make assumptions." I smiled again, but it was still fake. "And that'll be fun. It's been months since I've been truly hated around here."

"You may be overthinking it," he said with a steely calm that I didn't quite believe.

"Maybe," I conceded. "So, you want to talk feelings? Can we do it some other time, or does it have to be now?"

"We don't have to do it all now," he said, and I thought maybe I'd get off the hook easy. "But I have a few questions for you. Doesn't make sense to walk all the way back to my office, though, so we can do it here, if you'd like."

"Sure," I said with excessive pep. "Let's get it done."

"Your aunt?" He stared at me with those shrewd eyes, and I wondered if Scott had told him, or if he'd found out secondhand through Ariadne. "Charlie, I believe her name was? She betrayed you?"

I licked my chapped lips and smiled, a little manic at the thought, probably a defense against the real emotion underneath. "Yep, she did. Big surprise, huh?"

"I'm guessing it was for you," Zollers said, and there was warmth in it. "Am I wrong?"

"Nope," I said, keeping it succinct and overly zesty. "You're not wrong. It was a big honking surprise. She saved my life from James – the Omega operative – and then she turned on me in about three shakes, when I started to put together some things."

"Some things?" he asked. "You mean about who she really was?"

I nodded and unbound my hair from the tight ponytail I had it in, stuck the hair tie in my mouth and bit down on it while I redid my ponytail. "That's right. About how she was a crazy psycho who would drain men for the fun of it, for the rush, or to get money or information. Sounded like she must have killed quite a few people. Just like James, actually," I said with a little thought, and that allowed me to skirt the edge of a really big emotion that burned inside – betrayal.

"Tell me about James," he said. "What happened?"

"He tried to kill me," I said, with a great, exaggerated shrug of my shoulders. "Not much else to tell."

"Before that," he said, not letting it go, but doing so gently. "You broke up with Zack?"

"That a matter of public record?" I turned away.

"Not really," he said. "But I got the gist of it from him when I talked to him in the medical unit. What happened?"

"What always happens," I said, walking back to the wall of weapons and admiring my distorted reflection in the blade of a curved sickle. "Things fall apart."

"What a classical answer," he said, and I caught snark. "But when that happens, it's because the center cannot hold, right?"

"You an English major or a psychiatrist?" I flashed him a sharp smile, like the reaper I had just turned away from.

"Maybe I'm both," he said. "Don't change the subject. You broke up with him. Why?"

"Because it was going nowhere." I took a deep breath, tried to use it to give myself a chance to think for a second. "Because there is no next level of relationship for Zack and me," I said. "And that matters."

"To whom?" he asked, polite. His hands were tucked behind him, his weight on one leg, totally casual.

"To the guy who stocks the vending machines around the campus," I said with snark of my own. "Do I really have to answer obvious questions?"

"You don't have to answer any questions you don't want to," he said without expression. "But you should maybe try, because I don't think the answer is as obvious as you think."

"It matters to me," I said coolly. "It matters to Zack."

"How much does it matter to you?"

"A lot," I said. "I'm not a nun, okay? I'm not super excited about spending my life close to a man and never being able to sleep with him. It…is desperately unsatisfying."

"So you pushed him away?" Relentless. Driving.

"Sure," I said, and went back to inspecting a pair of sais hung next to the sickle. I saw him in the reflection this time, not me.

"Because if you can't be wholly satisfied, why be with some-one?"

"Because maybe I'd keep him from being happy with someone else," I answered, and ran my finger down the blade. It was deceptive, and I cut myself, a little line in the flesh of my index finger that filled with blood, pooling at the end of the cut, turning into a droplet. I turned to look at him again. "Because maybe I'm sick of this false closeness, this feeling of everything-but-intimacy."

"Is sex your definition of giving your all?" There was genuine curiosity in his returned gaze.

I looked back to the blood on my finger, as it traced a line to my palm and began to gather there. "No."

"You were going to have sex with James, weren't you?" He held his distance, about twenty feet between us, and I stared at the blood gathering in my palm. "Would you have considered that giving him your all?"

"No," I said. "I would have considered it…" I felt a sting. "I don't know. I don't know what I would have considered it. Expedient, maybe."

"It would be expedient to sleep with a man you didn't really know, just because you could?"

I didn't hear any judgment from him, but there was worlds of it in my head. "Right after I broke up with my boyfriend, you mean?" I didn't whirl at him; I kept composed. "Not even twenty-four hours later? What you must think of me."

"I don't think anything bad of you," he said, soothing.

"How can you not?" I asked, and laughed just a little, but again, manic. I felt the first stutter of emotion I'd been holding back since before I'd seen Andromeda bleeding, the red circle radiating out on her chest. "I am death. I get people killed, Doc. I couldn't stand that I couldn't be close to my boyfriend, so I pushed him away, broke up with him, then I went to a bar that very night, got drunk, and would have slept with a man who worked for the enemy, because I could." I said it with gusto, almost relishing the buildup of torturous emotion, like I was enjoying thrusting a knife into my own midsection and savoring the twist. "If Kat hadn't stopped me, I would have. And after that, my aunt betrayed me, my mother left me – again! And I got another person killed." I pictured Andromeda's youthful face, her wet and tangled hair, as she'd looked when I held her, as she died. She wasn't any older than I was. I broke into a laugh that turned into a half-sob. "How can you not think awful things of me? My own mother…" I felt my face twist. "She didn't take *me* with her."

There was a certain growing alarm on his face. "You can't think—"

"How can I not?" I held my hands apart, and felt the blood drip off my palm to the floor. "Not only am I good at getting people killed and driving others away, but my own mother—"

I stopped as I saw movement behind the windows. There was a man coming down the hall. Tall, balding, lean and wearing a suit with a white shirt and red tie. My eyes traced him as he came along, his demeanor straitlaced. He stopped at the glass door and it swung open.

"Time's up, Doc," he said with excessive casualness. "She'll have plenty of time for a counseling session later, but I need to talk with her now. Ariadne's orders." He nodded to me. "Come on."

Doc Zollers didn't turn to look at him, just stood there still fixated on me. "Mormont, I need a few more minutes—"

"Now," Michael Mormont said, not harsh, but without an ounce of give. "Come on, Nealon."

Zollers wheeled, and walked his way to Mormont, who watched him with a wary eye, and I saw him whisper something into Mormont's ear. I'm a meta, so I heard it too. "She's vulnerable right now," Zollers said, "and I need to help her through some trauma. I just need a few more minutes."

Mormont leaned in and whispered back. "She's vulnerable? Good. Then she'll answer my questions without fighting me as hard as her reputation leads me to believe she normally would." He slapped the doctor on the back and I saw a grin that was almost a sneer. "Don't worry, Doc. You're a master. You can pick up the pieces when I'm all done." With a finger he beckoned to me, and I caught the look from Zollers, the uncertainty.

I walked, one foot after another, toward him, passing Zollers, shrugging off the arm he tried to put around me, and out the door that Michael Mormont held open for me, into the hallway, where the cold of the air conditioner seemed overwhelming for some reason.

Chapter 9

Still bleeding, I walked out of the building, at which point I let Mormont cross in front of me. He shot me a sidelong glance as he passed, and I caught a glimpse of his smooth skin, not even a hint of five o'clock shadow on his face. His eyebrows were heavier, and his face held a bit of a smirk that he flashed me as he passed. He turned his back to me as he led me across the campus, following the paths that cut through the grass.

If there was anything I appreciated about Michael Mormont thus far, it was that he didn't try to make small talk on our walk to the headquarters building. He walked in front of me, self-assured enough that he didn't once look back to make sure I was following him. For my part, I wondered if I could blame it on Wolfe if I clubbed him from behind and ran off.

The sun was hot overhead, but I barely noticed, as it felt good against my sweat-soaked skin. My hair was sticking together in strands, and I could feel it frizzing above my forehead, struggling against the ponytail. I could almost see to the other side of the campus from here, and I gazed longingly at my dorm and the shower I knew it contained, wondering when I'd be able to enjoy the warm recharge within it.

I desperately wanted a drink of water now, the sour taste of bad breath making me run my tongue over the interior of my mouth as if I could rub the bad flavor out. In the distance I could hear a lawnmower running as the ground crew went about the business of making the Directorate look fabulous. I wished I was one of them right now. It had to be less precarious, dangerous and insane than what I was currently doing for work.

When we reached the headquarters building, Mormont entered, triggering the handicapped automatic door without looking back. I suppose I should have felt honored or something that he was trusting me not to run, but instead I felt an almost creepy self-assurance from him, like I was some poor puppet in his thrall and subject to his will no matter what. Then I felt a rush of irritation that bled over the torrent of emotions that had been hammering at me only a few minutes earlier.

The lobby of Headquarters was an ornate, marbled affair, black with white-flecked overtones. The air conditioning hit me as I walked in, but I didn't feel much of the chill this round, even though I was still dripping in my own sweat. Mormont led the way to the staircase that curved up to the second floor and started up. I followed, taking the stairs at a leisurely pace, slowing down to see if he'd notice. He adjusted to match, I realized after a second, apparently in no hurry since he had me going along with him, dragging me like a magnet draws filings across a surface. Bastard.

He went on, down a hallway of white, doors on either side, taking me through a wide-open space of cubicles buzzing with activity. One of the walls of the room was windows that looked down on the lawn, giving me a clear view all the way to the garage. The ringing phones and chatter slowed not one iota as I passed through, though I caught a few eyes of workers dressed in business attire, men in suits and ladies in skirts and jackets. A few of them dressed like Ariadne, I thought, as we entered another hallway.

Three-quarters of the way down the hall, he stopped at a room and opened the door. Inside was a table with two chairs, and against the wall behind one of them was mirrored window. I wondered who was on the other side, if anyone. Ariadne? Old Man Winter? Who would have the joy of watching me square off with this guy?

He watched me as he held the door open and gave me a nod

of false courtesy as I entered the room. I immediately went to the nicer of the two chairs and sat down, even though it placed my back in front of the mirrored window. He eyed me as I did it, but didn't say anything, taking the lesser seat. He grabbed the yellow pad of paper from in front of me and slid it over to him, taking his time, giving me a last chance to read what was on it. I caught a glimpse, but not much, and it looked like a cursory summary of Scott's account of the mission.

"So, are you settling back in?" He reached into his jacket for a pen, his hand emerging with a nice black ballpoint that he proceeded to click three times, causing me to raise an eyebrow in annoyance that he noted with a smile.

"Oh gee," I said, "and here I thought that because we were able to make it across the campus without speaking, we'd tacitly agreed to just skip the small talk."

"I didn't give my agreement to that, tacit or otherwise," he said, looking down at his pad. "Answer the question."

"I'm settling in just fine," I said, "and thanks for asking." Some sarcasm, not much, compared to…uh…a teenage girl. Okay, maybe a lot.

"Let's start at the beginning, shall we?"

"We could start at the end," I suggested. "The part where I leave and you go back to sitting here, making intimidating faces in the one way mirror." I chucked a thumb at the glass behind me. "You know, if that's your thing."

"Tell you what," he said, "why don't we just start with the juicy stuff and work our way back to the mundane details." His eyes made their way up, and I caught the first sign of something unpleasant in the way he leered at me. "When you encountered James Fries – the second time, in Eau Claire…" He looked down at the pad, as if checking for some small detail. "…what did you discuss?"

"College football," I said, snotty.

"Oh?" He looked up. "Go on." He smiled. "What scintillating aspect of college football did you talk about?"

"We didn't," I admitted.

"So you were just being snide?" He smiled even wider. "Noted," he said, and made a mark on the pad. "How did the conversation go?" I felt the air pressure in the room increase tenfold.

"He told me he was there to recruit me from the Directorate, though he didn't say who he worked for at the time."

"That wasn't all, though, was it?" He peered at me across the table, eyes boring into mine. It was hot now. The air conditioner had to have stopped working. "I mean, we know how the story ends – you and he went back to your hotel room. So what happened next?"

"He showed me that he could touch my skin without getting hurt," I said, and the uneasiness grew. "And I realized he was an incubus."

"After which you went to your room," he said, looking at the pad, "where you remained until Katrina – Agent Forrest – informed you that Ariadne was on a conference call?"

"Yes."

Mormont clicked his tongue as he skimmed the page in front of him. "Could you describe what happened when you got into the room?"

"Well," I said, "we turned on the TV, and watched an episode of *The Vampire Diaries*."

His eyes came up again, half-lidded, skeptical. "I'm sorry. Was that another joke? I can't tell."

"You'd have to be humorless to do this job, I suppose, so that makes sense." I flashed him a tight, insincere smile of my own. "We started to undress, and before we finished, Kat knocked at the door."

He waited, looking at me as though trying to sift my guts right there in the interrogation room. "And at this point, you didn't mention anything about Directorate operations, anything that was going on?"

"I didn't know anything was going on other than that we were hunting someone who was assaulting convenience store clerks and that we'd stumbled onto Omega operations in Eau Claire that had some tie to the robber." I folded my arms, pulling them off the table, and leaned back, felt the top of the chair press into my back, smelled the cold mechanical scent of the processed air.

"You returned to your room and spoke with James Fries again." He looked up from the pad and tapped his pen against the yellow paper. "What did you tell him?"

"That I had to go." I let it out, forced it out. "That I had a mission. That I was heading east," I said with reluctance, mentally smacking myself not so much for admitting it to this stiff-collared douche as that I had done it at all.

"And he was at the Omega facility when you arrived?" Mormont looked from me to his notes. "This...Site Epsilon?"

"Yes."

"Did it occur to you..." He looked up again, and this time there was a kind of faux concern I desperately wanted to smack sideways off his face. "...that he might be an Omega operative when you gave him this information?"

"I didn't think so," I said, "but I acknowledged it was a possibility."

"I see. And when you got there, you were ambushed?" He stared at the paper. "Do you think perhaps when he realized where you were going that he summoned some additional Omega security?"

I froze. I hadn't considered that. "No. I mean, it's possible I guess."

"Possible." He had a semi-smile now. "Is it also possible that because you warned him, he was able to rally additional Omega forces in the forms of helicopters and sweep teams – the very ones that ambushed you after your escape, and caused the death of the subject Andromeda?"

I felt overly warm now. "Possibly, yes. But in my judgment—"

"I'm sorry to interrupt," he said, not sounding remotely sorry and on something of a roll, "but you'd been drinking twice in the previous two nights, all while active on a mission." He looked up at me. "Would you consider that to be good judgment or bad?"

I wanted to grind my teeth but felt I lacked the muscle control. Instead my mouth hung slightly open, and I felt a surge of emotion. "Not so good."

"And taking an Omega operative back to your hotel room," he said, now riveted, focused in on me, "was that good judgment or—"

"Bad," I said, not looking back at him. "Obviously."

"So you really weren't exhibiting the greatest judgment, were you?" His smile went slightly toothy, baring them like a predator, and I noticed a slight yellowing on them, probably from coffee.

I was caught in his stare, and I looked behind me again, to the cold glare of the mirror, the overhead fluorescent shining off it, my face visible looking over my shoulder. I looked stricken, that's the only way to describe it, and Mormont knew it. I saw him, watching me in the mirror, and I didn't bother turning back to answer him. "No," I said, only just above a whisper.

"So," he went on, back to the pad of paper that I wished I could burn, "your mother left you in the state in which your colleagues later found you?"

"Yes," I said, a deep, galling pain stirring inside. "She did."

"And what state was that?" His voice was slick, like oil, his words almost fluid in his delivery, as though they were simply sliding out of him.

"Beaten. Bloodied. Wrecked." I stared back at him with all the faux defiance I had left. "Between James Fries and my aunt, I was pretty much an immovable mess."

"I see," he said with a clicking of his tongue. "And two of these people – actually three, if we count your mother, who didn't hurt you but did leave you in said condition – were ones...you trusted in some way." He stared at the paper. "Your aunt wasn't an Omega operative? Just another random psychotic succubus?" he asked, as though it were expected. "You are aware that the incubus and succubus are the most shunned of all metas – the 'old world' attitude toward incubi and succubi?" He smiled. "They're not well-regarded among metas. Something about being able to drain souls with a touch tends to alienate you from others; makes you untrustworthy." He was grim in his delivery, and I caught the sub-text: he'd just finished drawing the line between the behavior of Fries, my aunt and my mother, and now he was connecting it neatly back to me.

"It's not exactly my favorite thing about myself," I mumbled.

He gave it a moment's rest, as though declaring silent victory for making me turn on myself. His eyes never left me. "Your mother went by the name Brittany Eccleston outside of your home. Do you know why that was?"

"I assume she was hiding from the people she used to work for," I said.

"You mean the U.S. Government, who might be curious about why she survived their metahuman policing agency's de-struction?" He wore a small smile. "Did she give you any indica-tion what she was at the Omega facility for?"

"I don't know," I said. "She just kicked Charlie's ass, acti-vated the control panel that set loose Andromeda and then left." I held my arms up in total exhaustion and uncertainty. "I don't know."

"Hm," he said with a nod. "A few things we can rule out, I think. First, she wasn't there for you." He delivered this line with a cold precision and a hint of a smile. "She left Gillette, Wyoming and committed a string of robberies on the way, and it was only by following her trail that you even found the Omega facility. So...it wasn't because you were there."

"Right," I said, my voice lower than a whisper. I felt a burning at my eyes, and I hated Michael Mormont right then, more than anyone ever.

"Tell me." He looked up from his pad again. "Where do you think she would go? Now that she's kidnapped your colleague?"

"I don't know," I said. "I didn't know where to look for her before and nothing has changed. If she's not at our house?" I shrugged. "I don't even know what she was doing in Wyoming."

"We've already looked over your house and have agents in place to make certain that if she returns there, we'll know about it." His answer was brusque, businesslike and...almost remorseless, like he was attacking me with it. "Andromeda," he said. "What she told you; repeat it for me. As close to word for word as you can, please."

"She said there was a traitor in the Directorate." I wasn't even able to look at him. "That was it."

"That was all?" He cocked an eyebrow. "Nothing else?"

"Some other stuff about...looking to her in the dark." I shook my head, so desperately ready to be done. "I don't know. I didn't understand what she was saying. It made no sense."

"It made no sense?" He looked at me, impassive. "Or it made no sense *to you*?"

"To me, I guess. To Scott, either. He was there when she said it." I tried to take the sting out of his words by tossing Scott in the mix, but the truth was that I felt numb, and fully to blame for things I hadn't even considered. The good news, if there was any, was that I wasn't responsible for the horrific numbers of Directorate agents that had died thanks to Omega. The bad news was that I was probably responsible for Andromeda's death. Everything I touch turns to death.

He stood, abandoning the pad, and circled around his chair. I thought about standing myself, but I felt a compelling lack of energy. "What do you think of her death?" I blinked at him, uncomprehending. "She'd just saved your life from James Fries, helped you escape the Omega compound, had promised to give you information that would give the Directorate a complete picture of Omega's operations." His hands clutched the back of his chair, and I saw his knuckles become more pronounced as he held on tighter to the scuffed wood. "What do you think of that, now that she's dead?"

"Obviously I'm disappointed," I said, not quite sure what he was looking for.

"Disappointed," he said with a nod. "Yes, I can imagine. You, who admitted you've been recruited by an Omega operative, whose mother kidnapped one of her teammates. Leaving aside any petty jealousies you might have had for Katrina—" his eyes sparkled as he said it – "all these coincidences seem…a little much, wouldn't you say?"

I stared back at him in raw disbelief. "My aunt's a psycho. My mother's a rogue. And I've got bad taste in men, apparently. You throwing in the idea that I'm a traitor to the Directorate into the mix?"

He slid his hand along the back of the wood chair. "Only a fool wouldn't suspect you at this point."

I should have brushed it off. If all the things that had happened the last few days hadn't happened, I probably would have. I'm Teflon. Nothing sticks to me; not emotions, not…nothing. I'm tough. My reputation at the Directorate is unsentimental, brutal, hard-working, unfeeling. I blinked back the emotion again. "Did Ariadne tell you to ask me this?" I blinked again. "Does she suspect me?"

He was cool when he answered, slick, and it came out easy. "Does she look like a fool?"

I bit back the obvious, stupid, fashion-oriented reply and also the one where I told him what he looked like. "You're not gonna ask me if I'm a traitor point blank and get it out of the way?" I felt my lip quiver and I hated myself almost as much as I hated him.

"If you're really spying on the Directorate," he said with the same smirk, "you'd just lie."

"Do I look like I'm in a fit state to lie right now?" I let the doubt slip into it, and my words came out hushed, bursting with all the emotion I was trying to cram down, the burning in my eyes and my throat.

"You look like someone in far, far over her head, Ms. Nealon," he answered. "I don't know if that makes you someone who would betray your employer or not." He didn't smile now. "But I will tell you this: you are being watched. Every hour of every day. If you are, in fact, working with Omega, or with your mother, I will find out. It's what I do." He believed every word he said. He leaned over again, grasping the chair in front of him, and the smile came back. "And I'm very, very good at what I do."

Chapter 10

The silence was pervasive as I left headquarters. I had been in the room with Mormont for longer than I thought; the sun, which had been overhead when I left the training facility, was now dipping lower in the sky. In Minnesota, in the middle of summer, it would not set until near nine o'clock tonight, but the shadows were growing long, though it was still hot.

My feet carried me out the front door and I realized not for the first time that I was covered in sweat; some dried, more fresh than should have been possible in an air-conditioned space like I had been in. My legs seemed to work only mechanically, each step sending mild shocks through my body as I slouched my way out the door. I was a mess, I knew it.

A hot breath of wind blew past that felt as though it had been warmed over the heat element of an oven. Even still, it was not enough to drag me out of my fearful, lethargic shuffle. I looked left and right, feeling more like a broken person than I could ever have wanted to admit to.

I didn't go back toward the dormitory, which surprised me. My feet carried me, taking a concrete path that went in the other direction, toward the woods that ringed the campus. I left the path as I neared the trees, not wanting to go back to my little room, with the little bed and little space provided by the people who now suspected me of betraying them. I felt a flash of anger – a HOW DARE THEY sort of indignation that fizzled a moment later. Of course they thought I was betraying them. My mother kidnapped one of their agents. I came within a few inches of sleeping with a man who works with an organization killing their people – our people. I'd think I was a traitor, too.

My steps carried me into the woods, past the start of the treeline. The sun cast shadows of the tree trunks in angled parallel lines on the pine needle-covered floor of the woods. Small green shrubs sprouted every few feet, but unpaved paths were cut through the woods for the Directorate staff to walk if they so desired, worn down by the tread of countless feet. Some of the meta kids, the teenagers who sheltered here, would sneak out on these trails for something they weren't allowed to do in the dorms. I wondered why I'd never been warned against it, and realized that they'd always treated me with kid gloves compared to the other metas, even the kids. Was that just because I was so powerful they were desperate to keep me, or was there something else in play?

I went on, into the woods, deeper as the space around the path grew more unkempt and less trod. Trampled brown-orange pine needles were everywhere, the dull gray dirt and sands beneath it holding me up to keep me from falling through the earth – which is how I felt. Like I would collapse and be swallowed up by the earth, and that the sky would fall down upon me and drive me through it. I'd failed, completely, in everything. I had been ridiculously irresponsible on the mission, had compromised us to Omega. Even if I hadn't gotten our agents killed in the field I had almost certainly been responsible for James allowing Omega to be positioned to kill Andromeda after her escape.

Andromeda. I felt my knees give out when I thought of her. There was something so different about her, and not just because she had been imprisoned in some bizarre containment cylinder that wasn't unlike the box I was intimately familiar with. There was something in her manner, so different, so alien, that reminded me of someone that didn't have a lot of social experiences. I could relate. Her powers may have made her different; her odd ability to read others would have made them nervous. She might have been an outcast. Like me.

My gloved hand was on the ground, holding me up as I lay there on my knees. I could feel the emotions racking my body, threatening to escape with violent force, and I tried to suppress them. I wanted to be strong, but I felt my limit, and it was miles back. I had screwed everything up. I imagined Zack's face, the only man I knew who had ever really cared about me, and remembered the look I'd seen on him in the medical unit – the hurt, the betrayal. Zollers had nailed it: I was the center, whether I wanted to be or not, and I had failed to hold, and everything was falling apart around me. The Directorate had entrusted me with a great responsibility and I had screwed it up completely.

I dragged myself to a nearby tree and put my back against it. I felt weak, barely holding back the raging tide of emotion that was threatening to wreck me. There were other things weighing on my mind, obviously – I didn't need Zollers to tell me that I had deep, unresolved mommy issues. I blinked my eyes tightly, squinted them shut. I leaned my head against the rough bark, felt the knots and grooves of it bite into the back of my skull. Part of me wanted to push back harder, like I did with everything else except my interrogation, apparently. "Why?" I whispered.

"Why what?" came a sharp voice that caused my eyes to shoot open in surprise. I blinked, twice, to be sure I was seeing what I thought I saw, and not some stress-based delusion. My mother stood before me, her hair back in a ponytail like my own, her face frozen in utter disdain. She stood only feet from me, no gloves, but a business suit and makeup giving her a drastically different look than when I had last seen her. "You're sitting out here, exposed, with your eyes closed." She looked at me with a narrowed gaze of her own. "You're oblivious to the world around you – you didn't even hear me approach you from behind. If I'd been an enemy, you'd be dead." She maintained her distance.

"What…" I looked around, as though hoping someone else was seeing what I saw. "Are you…really here?"

She rolled her eyes so hard her entire head bobbed as she looked up and over, as though she were following the path of an imaginary fly ball going over her. "Please tell me it's the drugs they have you on that are making you this dumb. I never trained you to be this undisciplined, this STUPID about your personal safety." She squinted at me. "Where's Andromeda?"

I blinked at her, again. "Wh…Andromeda? You're…not here for me?"

This time she bowed her head in deep annoyance. "I realize I can't punish you the way I used to, but could you at least…do me the courtesy…of answering my question." She strained at the last, the final part of her sentence coming out in a low, growling bark.

"She's dead," I said, whispering again. "They killed her. Omega killed her."

"What?" My mother's staid expression, perpetually ready to display annoyance as her sole emotion, broke and her eyes widened in shock. "They couldn't have killed her – they wouldn't have—"

"They did," I said, soft, the emotion drying me out, taking away my sarcasm. "One of their soldiers shot her, and would have shot me if not for—"

"No." She shook her head. "That's not Omega's style. They would have wanted her back, after what they did to—" She shook her head again, and I could see the emotions rushing over her face, as she snapped back to masking them, calm indifference returning. "I'm sorry, that can't be right."

"I saw her die," I said. I looked at her, and cocked my head. "Where's Kat?"

My mother's arms tightened, folded in front of her on the arms of her suit, which was a perfect match for something Ariadne would have worn. "Not here," she said. "Why do you ask?"

"Because she's my friend—"

"Don't lie to me, Sienna," she said, with a frank air of unconcern. "I've been watching you since you were a child; I can tell when you do it. She's no friend of yours. You don't even like her."

"I…I like her fine." I reeled slightly. "She…tries to be my friend. If she's not, it's not her fault, it's mine. And she's…my colleague."

"Deep concern for a co-worker?" She studied me with a frown. "I doubt it; not for the little cheerleader. No, it's something else." She stared at me, sifting into my soul as though she had her hands on me and was draining the answers out of me. She laughed, a short one that was mostly fake, and her arms uncrossed. "They think you betrayed them. Erich Winter thinks you're working with me."

"No," I said in a hoarse whisper. "He thinks I'm working with Omega."

My mother laughed, a real one this time, originating from deep inside. "Ohhh, that's a good one. I doubt he really believes that, though you certainly kicked up some suspicions fraternizing with James Fries. I hope you learned your lesson about that particular glass of rotten milk without giving the cow away for free."

I blinked. "Was that…are you talking about me sleeping with him?"

"I don't care whether you did or not," she said, voice cracking like a whip, telling me something else entirely different from her words. "I just hope you didn't make a stupid mistake that you'll regret for the next eighteen years."

I flinched at her words. "Are you…are you talking about…me?"

Her look turned from raging to wary in an instant. "I have to go."

"Why are you here?" I said, and felt my back press against the tree again. "Did you stop by just to insult me? To add a few more logs on the fires of my insecurities?" I blinked back the tears that had been long suppressed.

"No," she snapped. "I saw you go into the woods, and I followed you." She hesitated now, seeming as though she were torn. "I wanted to—"

Something whistled through the air above us and I felt a tingle. I was moving even as Mom's head was swiveling, looking around us for the threat. I knew, however, that it was coming from above, directly above, and without even thinking I acted, pushing her with both hands. The look on her face was pure shock, and she lanced out with a fist that hit me in the jaw even as she was falling. She hit the ground on her back and used her momentum to roll back to her feet.

I, on the other hand, felt the blow from above, the one that had been meant for her, hit me square in the back and fling me facedown to the ground. My chin, fresh from being hit by her fist, was slammed into a root, followed by my chest, knocking the wind out of me. Stars filled my eyes, the metaphorical sort which were really colored flashes of light in my experience. I saw my mother looking at me for a half-second, her mouth a flat line, before she turned and ran, leaving her high heeled shoes behind in a sprint to get away from the place where I lay.

I stared at her back until she receded from view, my head full of lightness, and my limbs trapped, immovable beneath a net of light that restrained me, hugging me to the earth. I decided not to fight the desire to go limp, preferring instead to just lay there, hoping that the earth really would swallow me, that the sky really would fall down – not a net from Eve Kappler, like what was keeping me down now. I waited, and I heard the footfalls of M-Squad a few seconds later. I felt strong hands reach down, hard like iron, and rip the netting away, and then twist my arm behind me.

I cried out and was pulled to my feet, Clyde Clary standing in front of me, his skin turned a black, rubbery color. It felt like metal. He was leering at me with his stupid grin and had my hand twisted behind me, locking it into place behind my back as he did the same with my other hand, effectively handcuffing me without needing actual handcuffs. "Lookee here," Clary said. "Caught her fraternizing with the enemy red-handed."

"If my hands are red, it's because you're cutting off the circulation to them."

"Loosen up, Clary," I heard another voice say, and I was spun about to face the speaker. Roberto Bastian looked back at me, his black, short-cropped military flattop standing out in the late day shadows. His browned skin looked sallow in the fading light, and his lips were puckered like he was holding back whatever he wanted to say to me. "No need to hurt her."

"We got her," Clary said, dumbstruck. "We got her talking to her mom, live and here. What, you want me to let her go?"

"She ain't going anywhere," Bastian said, and turned to look back at Headquarters, "so loosen up your grip. It ain't like you can't run her down and catch her if she tries to rabbit." He turned to face me. "And it's not a crime to talk to your mother, though obviously it doesn't look good. We're gonna have to take you to Ariadne," he said, speaking to me at last. "If you try to run..." He shook his head, almost sadly. "Just don't. Let's get this over with."

"What about Eve and Parks?" Clary said with a nod in the direction my mother had run.

A noise in the underbrush got us all looking, and a wolf slinked out, then stood up on its hind legs as it became a man. Its fur became clothing, the hair atop its head and face becoming a gray beard and a long, bushy mane. "Eve's aloft," Parks said, "but it's pretty clear Sierra got away. Managed to leap the fence and make it to a car. I called Ariadne and the helo's warming up, but it won't be up in time to catch her." He turned to look at me. "What's your story?"

I swallowed hard. "You wouldn't believe me if I told you."

"Try me," he said and gestured with a nod of his head to start walking toward the headquarters building.

"I just got done with the interrogator," I said as Clary put pressure on my arms and started me moving forward, "and I came out here by myself. My mom was apparently on campus to do something and said she saw me and followed me out here."

"Simple," Parks said. "Undetailed. She was definitely here. Why would I doubt it?"

"Because the coincidences are piling up," I said as Clary tugged on my arm, causing me a surge of pain. I looked at him and he grinned. "And the circumstantial evidence of my guilt is gaining more and more circumstances with every passing day."

Parks chortled, and I heard Bastian clear his throat. "True enough," Parks said, and lapsed into silence.

I considered the only fortunate part of this being that headquarters would be close to abandoned when I arrived, just as it had been when I left a few minutes earlier, the people who worked there already gone for the evening. I especially didn't want to face the thought of the people around the campus seeing me in such a state, looking like hell, my face and clothes dirty and even ripped in a couple places from my rough landing after being taken down by Eve's net. I looked down and saw smudges of brown dotting my grey t-shirt. I couldn't imagine what my face must look like, but I could feel some of the dusty grit on my forehead and cheek.

The route back to the headquarters building carried us past the dorms, and as Clary led the procession off the path and across the grass, I realized too late what he was doing. Bastian and Parks said nothing until we rounded one of the glassy corners of the building and I saw the boxy outline of the cafeteria and the shapes within. By then it was too late, and as I started to resist, Clary twisted my arm, urging me to go on.

"You are such an ass, Clary," Bastian said under his breath. Parks let out a hiss of breath to agree.

We walked past the cafeteria's massive, open glass walls, already committed to our path. Clary marched me on, my arms snugged behind my back in a prisoner-like state, my shoulders hunched and my frame bent so he could control my movement easier. I didn't look to my right as we passed the cafeteria. I didn't need to. It was dinnertime, and I had seen silhouettes behind the glass; people rising from their seats and coming to the window to look at me being led along by three members of M-Squad, like a felon, in front of pretty much everyone I knew.

The heat burned in my cheeks and I pushed down the tears again, this time of humiliation and rage, and I tried to quicken my pace, but Clary held me back now, and I heard a little guffaw from him as he slackened his tread to draw out my perp walk. "You having fun with this?" I asked him under my breath.

"Sienna girl, I am having as much fun as I could possibly be having. What's the matter?" he asked with a laugh. "You not enjoying your fifteen minutes of shame?"

"No," I said hoarsely. "No, I'm not."

He chuckled, a sound like a wheezing heifer. "Don't do the crime if you don't wanna do the time."

"Stifle it, Clary," Parks said.

"What are you getting all up in my grill for, Parks?" Clary said with disdain. "We caught her with a woman who broke into our facility."

"Talking, Clary," Parks said. "And nothing else that we could prove."

"Prove, schmove," he said. "She's guilty as hell."

They marched me through the heavy glass doors of the headquarters building, into the elevator, and we rode up, Clary still affecting his rubber form, keeping my arms locked in place. I felt it every few minutes as he would subtly increase the pressure on my arms. Not so much Parks or Bastian would notice, or enough to make me cry out, but enough to cause me pain. I wanted to hurt him, but even stomping as hard as I could on the instep of his foot (the preferred remedy for dealing with someone restraining you in such a way) would produce only more pain for me.

When the elevator doors opened, I stepped out and started toward Ariadne's office, flanked by the three of them. Her office was against outside windows. The windows that looked from the cubicle farm into her office had the blinds closed and when we reached the heavy wood door, Bastian stepped in front of me and knocked. He looked down at me from his six foot-plus height, and I caught a hesitancy that verged on remorse. He didn't say anything, though, and after a moment a voice called from inside for us to enter, and he opened the door.

Ariadne was standing behind her desk, her dull gray suit marked contrast to the orange cast of the world outside the window behind her. It was early evening now; the sun was sinking lower in the sky and on the other side of the building to boot, so most of the grounds were shadowed, the lawn dark in the shade of headquarters. Ariadne looked at me in surprise, blinked a few times, her gaze swinging from me to Clary, who was still clutching my wrists, and thunderclouds moved in over her brows. "Clary...what the hell are you doing?"

"Ma'am," Bastian said. "We caught up with her talking with her mother in the woods."

"Her mother?" Ariadne asked. "Her mother was the intruder?" She looked at me in sharp disbelief.

"Yes, ma'am," Bastian said. "Eve and Parks went after her, but she managed to get to a car and escape."

Ariadne stood in the middle of the office, her red hair a perfect match for the light on the trees in the background. "Clary, Bastian, Parks...out."

Clary tensed and I felt his grip tighten on my wrists. "But—"

"Out, Clary. Wait in the hall." She said it quietly but firmly. I heard Parks and Bastian move to comply. Clary was rooted in place, though, as if his brain couldn't quite process what he was been asked to do. "I'm not going to ask you again."

"She could be dangerous, you know," Clary said behind me, and I could hear the defensive heat in his voice. "What if she kills you and makes her escape out the window?"

"Then you'll have a really fun time smearing her all over the campus," Ariadne said, as though indifferent to the prospect.

Clary seemed to ponder this for a minute before I felt his hands release my wrists. "Oh. Huh. Yeah, that'd be fun." His heavy footfalls cut a path out the door behind me.

"You want me to leave, too?" I heard a voice behind me and turned my head to see Reed in the corner, leaning against the wall, looking pretty dapper for a guy who'd been out of it when last I'd seen him. He was wearing a black suit and his dark hair was up in a ponytail, a splash of color from his collared dress shirt, which was pink. It actually looked good on him.

"You can stay," Ariadne said, remaining standing. I realized, not for the first time, that Ariadne was taller than me. She never really felt that way, though, for some reason. She stared at me, and I stared back, and neither of us said anything.

"Well, gosh," Reed said, "with this being such a great, not-at-all-awkward moment, that's an awfully enticing offer, but why don't I just go ahead and mingle with metal head and the M-Rejects while you two hash out whatever dramatic tension you've got." He slipped behind me and opened the door, shutting it behind him.

I stood there, bedraggled, haggard, a torrent of emotions still buried. I didn't want any of them bleeding out now, or in the presence of any other person, come to it. "Sit down," Ariadne said, gesturing to the chairs in front of her desk.

"I don't think I'll be doing your upholstery any favors," I said, massaging my wrists where Clary had twisted and clamped on them. They ached, but they were the least of my problems. I tasted blood in my mouth and a pain on my tongue told me I'd bitten it when I hit the ground, though I hadn't noticed at the time. I was sticky from old sweat and my jaw hurt, along with the rest of my body, a half-dozen aches reminding me that Eve hadn't been gentle with her application of the net. I guess I hadn't earned much goodwill with her, though, if I thought about it.

"Sit," she said, and this time it was quiet, no order, just a gentle invitation, absolutely at odds with what I thought I'd get from her.

I sat, lowering myself into the faux black leather. I felt it hit my back awkwardly, as though it was forcing me into better posture than I wanted to adopt at the moment, making me sit upright when I wanted to slouch and play wounded, wanted to keep out of eye contact so she couldn't delve into me and see how hurt I was by everything that had occurred.

"What happened?" she asked me, taking her own seat and causing her chair to squeak at the wheels as she slid it to move closer to the desk.

I pursed my lips. "I got done with my meeting with Mormont and went to the woods for a few minutes to just…" I paused, trying to find a way to cover what I really wanted to say, which was to be alone and cry where I hoped no one would see or hear me. "…try and gather my thoughts. My mom said she saw me walking across the campus."

"What did she say to you?" Ariadne's eyes were rimmed with concern, and I couldn't tell in my present state whether it was real or not. My bullshit detector was broken, along with the rest of my emotions.

"She asked me where Andromeda was. I told her." I thought again of Andromeda, who had saved my life, and how I couldn't do the same for her. I wished I had taken the bullet and not her. "I asked her about Kat and she evaded." I felt a shudder as I thought about how Mom had treated me when she wanted to restrain me. "She ripped me a new one about being lax in my habits. Same old story." There was a gap of silence after that, and I didn't want to break it, so I stayed as stoic as I could, even as I turned over the insults my mom had hit me with in the few minutes I had talked with her.

"Michael Mormont gave me his recommendations of what we should do with you while he continues his investigation," Ariadne said, breaking the silence. She had her fingers palm down on the desk, and stretched out in front of her on the black surface.

"Draw and quarter me?" I suggested. "A public flaying? Whipped naked through the campus at noontime?"

"He recommends we take you into custody," she said softly, and I didn't react. I didn't know if I had it in me to even try to run, assuming I had anywhere to go other than my house, where they would surely catch me in less than an hour. "But I want you to know," she said, catching my attention even as I felt my body slacken, as though I could slide out of the chair like the emotional jelly that I was by this point, "that the Director and I have discussed it, and we've discarded his recommendation. We don't believe you're the traitor."

I felt a slight warmth, amazement, and felt a choked sensation in my throat. "But...what about all the things that have gone wrong...James...and I mean...what I did..."

"Mistakes," she said, soft again, "not malicious." She pursed her lips. "But we trusted the three of you to get the job done when we sent you on assignment, one that ended up evolving into something of vital importance at a time when we're under more pressure than ever before, and we find you've been drinking on the job and...taking random men back to your hotel room who turn out to be spies for our enemy." She said it softly, like everything else, and it wounded me even worse. "Do you have anything to say for yourself?"

I coughed, fake. I needed to clear my throat. "I don't have anything that doesn't sound in my head like an excuse."

"I'm disappointed," Ariadne said. "I guess I'd come to expect more out of you than this."

"You didn't even want me to go on this assignment," I said quietly. "Remember? You were still holding a grudge from when I took Eve out of the air with a rock."

"I wasn't holding a grudge," she said. "Scott is immature and acts like it. Kat's a sweetheart, and she'll go along with whatever he says because they're attached at the..." She blushed. "...because they're attached. But you," she said, and leaned forward, fingers interlaced, "you always marched to your own tune. Since the day you got here, you've consistently been one of the strongest metas not only in power, but in personality, weathering adversity I couldn't imagine." I could see by the look on her face she was telling the truth. "You never let it weigh you down, and you never followed anyone's orders if you didn't want to do something. You'd let the whole Directorate hate you before you caved on doing something you didn't believe was right. Remember Gavrikov?" She stared at me. "So I sent *that* girl out on an assignment, and when she didn't show up, I guess it surprised me."

"I can do better," I said. "I'm sorry."

"I know you can," she said sadly. "And I hope you get a chance to prove it. I know you hate me, but the Director and I have invested a lot of faith in you. I just hope it pays dividends at some point." She looked down. "But right now it's not looking too good."

I started to respond, I did. I wanted to say something about how bad I'd screwed up, about how much my judgment had been off, and how I really didn't hate her. But I waited a moment too long and there was a knock at the door. "Come in," Ariadne said, and the door opened to show a small, geeky guy with glasses and kind of a bowl-shaped haircut that reminded me of pictures I'd seen of the Beatles. He was wearing hipster glasses, which I hate. Unkempt, a ragged overshirt with holes in it covering a t-shirt underneath with the name of some band on it I doubted anyone had heard of.

"J.J," she said with a nod. "Progress?"

"Big time," he said with a smile, and stepped into the office.

"Just a second," she said, and looked out the door behind him. "Reed, you can come back in now."

Reed appeared at the door, sliding into the room unmussed and without a word. He resumed his place in the corner and I watched a cell phone slip into his pocket from one of his hands. He really did look good in the suit, but his persona was off somehow; I realized after a moment his expression was guarded, more closed than I'd ever seen before from him.

J.J., as Ariadne had called him, sat in the seat next to me, a tablet computer in his hands. Tufts of cat hair streaked his dark blue skinny jeans. "So, the basics of what they did here were a deeper encryption than just relying on the normal OS security protocols—"

"J.J.," Ariadne said, "I don't care about that. What did you find on the computer?"

"Wait," I said. "Is this about the laptop I recovered from the Omega safehouse?"

"Right," the hipster geek said with a nod. "I've made sure it was clear of spyware, tied it into the network, and backed the contents of the hard drive up onto our servers so you can access it from your computer." He waved to the laptop on the work hutch behind her. "But here's the gist: a list of U.S. Assets for Omega – though they don't quite call themselves that on their internal docs," he said. "It's kinda vague, but I got some analysts sifting through it now. Looks like street addresses for safehouses, facilities, the works. Some names of employees."

"Anything in the immediate area?" She looked at him and his gaze popped up from the tablet computer.

"A guy here in Minneapolis," J.J. replied. "James Fries?

Looks like they're paying for him to live the high life; he's got a condo in downtown."

"And I would love to visit and throw him out of a window to show my gratitude," I said.

"And wouldn't defenestration be a simplistic approach?" Ariadne said with a raised eyebrow. "One incubus dead on the Omega side isn't going to win us this war. I'll put surveillance on him, see if he leads us anywhere interesting."

"And then, after you've done that, I can...?" I mimicked throwing something over my head. I didn't mean it, not really – I don't think.

"We've got bigger concerns than revenge," Ariadne said, but her look was muted sympathy. "We've got a final tally of over a hundred and eighty dead nationwide – that's agents, retrievers, metas and all else."

"That doesn't sound too bad," J.J. said with a shrug. I didn't like him.

"That's about three-quarters of our agent assets," Ariadne said. "And every one of them had people they left behind – mothers, fathers, wives, husbands, kids in some cases..."

"Oh," J.J. said in muted surprise. "Well, when you put it like that it sounds bad."

"Could be worse," Reed grunted from the corner, drawing my attention back to him. A pall hung over him, a blackness of mood I couldn't quite place, it was so at odds with the flippant guy I'd known since he offered me a ride after knowing him for ten seconds.

"How?" Ariadne asked, slight amusement causing the corners of her mouth to curl in a faint smile.

"You could be a meta in India," he said without pause. "Their government has been running a training facility like what you've got here, where they've been sheltering metas – about four hundred of them. They've even been taking them in from other neighboring countries with offers of good money and a high standard of living."

"That doesn't sound so bad," J.J. said with a shrug. "Working for the government would have some benefits, I'm sure. Like maybe some past indiscretions could be evaporated without having to do a hack job—"

"They're all dead as of this morning," Reed said darkly. "Every last one of them."

"What?" Ariadne's eyebrows arched up and she sat back in her chair, stunned.

Reed seemed to seethe with pent up energy in the corner, every word coming out as though he were about to explode. "They're dead. The whole compound was destroyed."

J.J. seemed to maintain a detached, ironic tone. "Did their government wipe them out? Because that's not cool."

"No," Reed said, staring at J.J. in disbelief. "That would not be 'cool'," he said, mocking the techie. "But indicators do not point to the Indian government."

"Omega?" I asked, and traded a look with Ariadne.

"Don't know," Reed said, "but it doesn't sound like their game. I don't know if you knew this, but about six months ago in China—"

"Right." Ariadne seemed to awaken, leaning forward. "That Chinese government facility that was destroyed."

"Taking three hundred plus metas along with it," Reed agreed. "This hasn't been a good year for the meta population. We're down by nearly eight hundred in the last few months, and there were only about three thousand of us to begin with."

"Why would you put all your metas in one place?" J.J. mused aloud. "I mean, it just seems like an invitation to get them wiped out."

"No one thought we were in any danger of extermination until now," Reed said with a little acrimony. "Our reports out of China were vague; there was even a hint it could have been the Chinese government behind the whole thing." He blinked and turned his head toward the wall. "Doesn't look like it now, though. Looks pretty much like an outside job."

"So someone's wiping out metas?" Ariadne asked, sitting back again. "I mean, if China was an isolated incident, you might be able to write it off as an isolated occurrence, but…" She looked at Reed. "How did you get this information?"

"I just talked with my superiors in Italy," Reed said. "They were…hesitant to give me much over an open communication source like a cell phone, but…anyway, I got the basics and gave them an update." He shook his head. "The good guys seem to be in a spiral here. Feels like we're fighting blind. I sense they know something about the troubles you're experiencing, but I'll need to call from the secure line at my apartment to get the full updates."

Ariadne stared at Reed. "Why don't you go do that?"

Reed smiled. "Because my apartment is in Milwaukee."

"Damn," I said. "How the hell do you keep up with your HQ when you're on the road?"

"Well," he began, "we had cell phones that we thought were unbreakable – until about six months ago, when we caught an Omega spy in Florence who had a copy of our encryption protocol on him."

"They're starting to seem rather adept at this sort of penetration," Ariadne said. "They've compromised us as well; Andromeda claims we have a traitor in our midst."

Reed nodded. "Doesn't surprise me. Omega is very slick, and they've got more than a few teeps on their side to deploy for these purposes."

"I'm sorry," I said, confused. "What's a teep?"

"TP," Ariadne said, drumming her fingernails on the desk. "Telepath. Mind readers. How many do they have?"

"No idea," Reed said with a shrug. "No names, no certainty;

just whispers, rumors that they use them for spying."

"Oh wow," J.J. said. "So we've got people walking around reading our minds?" He twitched. "Ah…can I have some time off until we get this resolved? I mean…I've got information that they really shouldn't have, after all. I could work from home."

I looked at him seriously. "Is it about your unhealthy relationship with your cat?"

His eyes widened and his jaw dropped open, making him look even more ridiculous than his glasses and haircut already did. "How did you know about my cat?" He blinked. "Are you the mind reader?" He whimpered. "It was only the once, I swear."

I let out an exhalation. "You're covered in cat hair…" I looked at him in pity. "…and ew. Ew. A thousand times, ewww."

Ariadne stared at J.J. as he wilted in his chair, then turned back to Reed. "Why don't you let us fly you to Milwaukee? We could use your organization's assistance and whatever information they have, if they're willing to provide it."

Reed considered her offer for about a second. "I'll take you up on that. Flight time is a hell of a lot better than a six-hour drive each way. I'm sure they'll be willing to render some help because I've been told to cooperate with you; it's just a question of how much. I mean, it's pretty obvious we've got some common enemies here."

"Though they're becoming more uncommon by the minute," J.J. said.

"Nice," I said with a glare. "Did you come up with that one all by yourself, Catman?"

"Go ahead, Reed," Ariadne said, picking up her phone. "I'll have a chopper spun up and ready to fly within the hour." She looked to J.J. and then to me. "I think we're done here, unless either of you has anything else to cover?"

"I'm good," J.J. said. "But seriously, can I work from home?"

"No," Ariadne said and started to dial numbers. "And Sienna?" She caught my gaze as I was standing. "Try and stay out of trouble," she said as gently as she could manage.

I followed J.J. and Reed out the door, and watched techno-hipster make his way through the maze of cubicles. Parks and Bastian were engaged in a conversation, Clary lurking next to them, trying to act like he was involved in it as they both studiously ignored him. Eve stood behind them at a distance, coolly watching. When I emerged from the office she walked toward me. I locked eyes with her and she with me. The scarring on her head and face had faded since last I saw her, although she looked odd without hair. She made a move to shoulder check me out of the way so she could enter Ariadne's office, but I evaded her with quick footwork and gave her a cold look in return. She let a cruel smile show, flashed at me along with a pointed finger that she proceeded to wag. "What do you want us to do with this one?" she asked Ariadne, and kept her finger aimed at me.

"Leave her be," Ariadne said. "Can you come in and shut the door?"

"You want us to come in, too?" Clary called from his place next to Parks and Bastian, craning his head and leaning to look in the open door of Ariadne's office. Bastian shook his head, eyes closed, and Parks let out a sigh. Clary didn't notice. Eve, for her part, remained still, back against the doorframe.

"No," Ariadne said. "I just need to talk to Eve."

She walked into Ariadne's office and shut the door behind her. "What?" Clary said, responding to something either Parks or Bastian had said that I didn't hear. "Ohhhh." The big man nodded, and a wide smile crept over his face. "Right."

"What the hell is wrong with that guy?" Reed asked me as I followed him toward the elevator bank. He tossed his thumb over his shoulder toward Clary with a perplexed-bordering-on-irritated look on his face.

"A lot," I said, not looking back. "What do you think of this

India thing?"

"I'm fine, by the way," Reed said, pushing the button for the elevator. "In case you were wondering."

I looked him up and down. "You seem to be doing better than me, that's for sure. Very slick." I held up my hands. "No need to get all snooty; if there's one of us standing here that looks like they're not doing well, I don't think it's you." I waved my hand up and down to encompass him from head to foot.

He cracked a smile. "You're tough. I'm sure you've faced worse."

I let out a breath. "Doesn't feel like it today. Today makes me wish I'd taken you up on that offer to visit your employer." He started to say something but I waved him off. "Don't say it. I'm not that serious about it."

"So what happened?" The elevator dinged and he indicated I should go first. The mirrored back wall of the elevator gave me a look at myself. I was smudged with dirt from top to bottom, my nose had blood underneath it, and there were a few scrapes visible on my face that I hadn't realized were there. Nothing too deep, but enough that blood was visible beneath them. They'd all be gone by morning.

"My mom snuck onto the campus, unleashing all sorts of pandemonium for me because they caught me talking to her," I said, dabbing at my nose with my sleeve. It came back with droplets of blood. "Now I'm under suspicion of betraying the Directorate."

"You know," he said after a pause, "you could come with me."

"I said 'don't say it'." I dabbed again. The blood had started to dry and crust on my upper lip. My eyes were red, though not from excess crying, because I'd barely shed more than a single tear. More likely from restraining it. "I'm in enough trouble right now without adding another reason to think I'm a traitor. God knows what the investigator would think about this conversation if he heard it."

"Investigator?" Reed cocked an eyebrow at me.

"Yeah," I said. "They're trying to root out the spy."

"And they were questioning you because you knew who this person was?" He eyed me, and I saw a little cold fire in his eyes, and caught it in his tone.

I turned to him and gave him a patronizing look. "My mom is the Directorate's Public Enemy Number Two right now, and I almost slept with the closest thing to a face we have for their Public Enemy Number One."

"I agree that gives you a slight air of suspicion—"

"Air?" I snorted and turned back to the mirrored wall, pushing at a scabbed cut in my eyebrow. "Reed, I think that qualifies as a cloud of suspicion, but a big one, like the kind you'd find surrounding a hurricane."

He didn't answer, and the elevator chimed as the doors slid open, revealing the marbled floors of the lobby and a darkening sky beyond the glass windows and doors at the front of the building. "Maybe," he conceded, "but I don't buy this idea that you're betraying the Directorate."

"Neither do Ariadne and Old Man Winter, apparently," I said as I stepped out into the open lobby. "But I wouldn't blame them for at least harboring some suspicions because of it."

"Don't let it get you down," he said with a muted smile and put a hand on my shoulder, shaking me slightly.

I looked at his hand as though it were contaminated and he froze. "Thanks, dude," I said sarcastically. "I can tell you totally mean that, bro." His eyes widened, and he stammered. "Sorry," I said. "I probably came on a little strong with that one. I just meant…" I closed my eyes and shook my head. "I appreciate you trying to cheer me up."

"Yeah." He kind of wobbled. "Well. Um. I will see

you…when I get back from Milwaukee, I guess."

I raised an eyebrow. "If this was a horror movie, I'd tell you to rethink that last line – it's pretty close to 'I'll be right back'." I thought about it for a second. "Actually, my life has resembled a horror movie in a few details lately. You might want to rephrase that."

"I'll be fine," he said with a roll of the eyes. "But I do want to talk to you about something when we have a little more time."

"It better not be a recruitment offer," I said, "because if it is, I swear to you—"

"It's not," he said. "I'll see ya later, okay?"

"There you go again."

He laughed and pulled his hand back into the elevator as the doors slid shut behind him.

My walk across the campus was long. It was evening now, the sun close to setting, glaring at me from the horizon with an orange stare. I shuffled back to the dormitory building ignoring the looks I got from the few people still making their way around the campus. It was worse when I entered the building; dinner was wrapping up and I caught stares and gazes from a dozen people, none of whom I really knew. The whispers were mostly inaudible but totally comprehensible; and I didn't even bother to enter the cafeteria where the smaller dinner crowd could have an opportunity to talk about me while I sat by myself and pretended to ignore it. I was edgy enough I might not have pretended, actually, and the last thing I needed was to get into a fight with someone right now.

The air conditioner was working overtime in the hallway to my room, blowing cold air out of the overhead vents as I walked down the hall, windows to the sunset-tinged campus on one side and plain white walls on the other. I was so hungry that I felt my mouth drool at the smell of food from the cafeteria, but I knew I'd have to be contented with whatever snacks I had in my room. The aroma of beef told me they were having that oh-so-rare treat, prime rib, but there was no way I was going to brave the lunacy of the crowds tonight, even for that. Besides, I could still hear the crowds in the cafeteria, and they didn't sound quiet: they were boisterous, there was discussion (probably about me), and I wanted no part of it.

I opened the door to my room, which, as usual, was unlocked. I had grown used to the small print of S. Nealon on the door's name plate, as though anyone who didn't know couldn't just look at the directory in the main hall entry to the dorm building. I didn't have anything worth stealing, just the Directorate-issued stuff that everyone else had in their rooms, so I usually didn't bother locking the door. Part of the reasoning for that was because I really sucked at keeping track of things like keys, so I didn't want to have to carry a key with me all the time just so I could lose it every day.

I came in and shut the door behind me, letting the back of my head thud against it. My day had consisted of waking up in the medical unit, telling my bosses (and inadvertently my ex-boyfriend) that I'd nearly slept with the enemy, getting to see one of my colleagues vent his righteous rage against my mother, getting interrogated by my psychiatrist (sad that I need one of those) then an actual interrogator (sadder that I'd need one of those); then I capped everything off by getting insulted by my mother, restrained by my co-workers, perp-walked in front of everyone I know, and then lectured by a woman who acts more like my mother than the real one. Best. Day. Ever.

Oh, and Kat was still missing. Joy. I bet she had a better day than me. I frowned and thought of the box. Maybe not.

I flipped the light after standing there for a minute in the dark, and I took my first uneasy steps toward the bed. I stopped, and cocked my head, curious, at a small object lying on the bedspread. I took a few steps forward and bent over to take a closer peek.

It was a watch. A gold band with links gave way to a clasp, and the face was kind of pearlescent, with a rainbow sheen that refracted in the light as I picked it up. The numbers on the face were roman numerals. At the three o'clock position was a number for the day, and the second hand was ticking along, counting out each moment as I stared at it. There was a shred of paper threaded beneath the band, and I looked to my desk; it was from the pad there, torn out, and something had been written on it. I pulled it out and opened it at the fold, blinking as the words registered in my mind, sticking there, sending my head into an even worse spin than it had already been in.

Your father would want you to have this.

Chapter 11

I lay down on my bed after that, staring at the watch for hours. It had no identifying markings on it, nothing that would have told me anything about its owner save for the note. I didn't recognize the handwriting, but in fairness it was a total scrawl, like it had been written in block print by a hand in one hell of a hurry. Which made sense, because whoever it was had been in my room uninvited, and thus subject to trouble from Directorate security if caught. So, probably my mother.

I placed the watch on my wrist and stared at it. It was huge compared to my slender arm and there was probably an inch of space in the diameter of the band. I let it spin loosely, playing with it, wondering if it was really his, and who he was. I read the note over and over. It said my father *would* want me to have it. Did that mean he was dead? Or somewhere he couldn't be reached? I blinked, and I felt the stir of emotions that had dogged me all day.

Did he think about me? Had he ever even seen me? Did he care?

I let the tears slip down my cheeks, but I muffled the sobs as best I could with my pillow. They were soft, quiet as I could make them, afraid that the thin walls were working against me in this regard. I felt the cool lines that each tear made, from the blurriness around my eyes down the sides of my face and temples to the bed where I lay. After a few minutes I moved my head and realized that the bedspread was soaked on either side of my cheeks.

I fell asleep for a little while, feeling sorry for myself, and I only knew that because I awoke with a start to knocking on my door. I sat up, breathing heavy, dazed, having come out of a deep, dreamless sleep. I sprang to my feet and went to the door, opening it in a rush. It was night, black outside the windows, and I knew that knocks on the door at this hour, whatever it was, could be nothing good.

Zack stood outside my door, grim, dark circles under his eyes, his suit completely askew. He looked mussed, way worse than usual, and I'd seen him after just waking up. This was not like him at all. "Ariadne needs us now," he said, all business, and started to turn away.

"What?" I asked, still trying to fully awaken.

"Reed's helicopter went down near Prescott, Wisconsin," Zack said, turning back.

"Oh," I breathed, a pain in my midsection like someone had kicked me in the gut. "That jackass just had to tempt fate."

I followed Zack, who was already walking back toward the entrance. We met Scott and Kurt coming from the opposite hall-way, the dorms on the other side of the building. Scott looked a lit-tle dazed, and his curly hair was flattened on one side from what I assumed was him sleeping on it. Kurt had a slight limp, and still bore bandages on his face from the car wreck.

"You look like hell," Scott said to me as we met up in the lobby, all four of us striding purposefully out of the front doors and onto the warm night air that blanketed the campus.

"You should talk, Flock of Seagulls," I replied with a little zing that sent him reaching for his hair and finding it plastered in place.

"You're both too young to even know what Flock of Seagulls is," Kurt said with a shake of his head. "Were you even alive in the 80s?"

"Wait, were they an 80s band?" I asked. "I just thought he looked like that guy in Pulp Fiction."

There was already a Black Hawk helicopter waiting for us on the landing pad outside headquarters. The rotors started to spin the moment we got into sight, and Ariadne was there, along with a couple other agents. The noise from the rotors was far too loud for conversation, but I saw them loading things into the side doors, and I suspected that we wouldn't be going unarmed.

Ariadne nodded to me as I ducked (I was so short I probably could have walked full upright without worrying about being decapitated, but when a helicopter rotor is swinging overhead, you don't think about these things logically) and climbed up into the chopper. I adjusted the five-point harness restraints and pulled a headset from under my seat. I put it on to muffle the rotor noise as I watched the agents that had been waiting with Ariadne shut the doors. The minute they were closed I felt the pilot throttle up and we were airborne, lifting into the sky and in motion, heading east.

"The helicopter went down about twenty minutes or so from here." I could hear Zack talk through the speakers in the headset. "We got a call from the pilot that said they were attacked."

"Where's M-Squad?" I asked, the first question popping into my mind.

"Parks was on the chopper," Zack replied. "Clary and Bastian were sent out on a quick mission to North Dakota to provide escort for a couple of our agents near Fargo, trying to get them home safely after they got bushwhacked by Omega. And Eve is remaining at the Directorate to keep an eye on things in case Omega is trying to draw us out."

"Faulty logic," Scott said, shaking his head. The plastered hair still didn't move, even with his vehement action. "If they're trying to draw us out, we should bring everything we've got and hit them hard."

"I think he means that Eve's going to provide defense for the campus in case they're trying to draw us out to hit it," I said, and a look of, "Oh, yeah," went across Scott's face.

"Makes sense, doesn't it?" Zack said with a tight smile. "After all, there are more metas at our campus than anywhere else in

North America."

"Wait, what?" Scott looked up in surprise. "I thought the Directorate had six campuses in the U.S."

"They do," Kurt responded, sounding like he was educating this snot-nosed punk, "but ours is the training center. All the young metas we're harboring, M-Squad, you kids – there are almost a hundred on the campus. You oughta know that. The other campuses act as feeders and locations for mostly human agents and retrievers to work out of. Once they identify a prospect, they get sent here. Unless they're a threat," he said. "Then it's off to—"

"Arizona," I finished for him. "How many metas are there in North America?"

"More than you'd think," Kurt answered, looking at me across the darkened compartment. "We estimate no less than five hundred."

"Is that...a lot?" Scott asked.

"Considering there were probably only five hundred or so in India and China, yes," Kurt said with calm uncaring.

"Why is that?" Scott asked as my mind hummed along, wondering what we were about to walk into.

"If you've got abilities that unbalance the scales of life," Zack said, "wouldn't you use your advantage to put you in the most prosperous place you could? Metas come to America and western Europe in higher numbers from everywhere else in the world. Plus, with longer lifespans, they have a higher likelihood of making it here eventually."

One of the two agents who had stood with Ariadne was rummaging in a duffel bag. He came out with an HK MP5 submachine gun and handed it to me with a smile. I nodded at him in thanks, and realized it was Jackson, the guy we'd found when my mother kidnapped Kat. He was dark haired, and had a tactical vest over a white dress shirt. He handed me a tactical vest of my own and I unstrapped myself to put it on while he gave the same to Scott, then Kurt and Zack. I checked my submachine gun to make sure a round was chambered and then made sure the safety was on. I kept it pointed down and right, toward the door, the way Parks had drilled it into my head.

"What are we looking at here?" I asked.

"Chopper went down near Prescott after a tightband mayday that went direct to us," Zack said. "It was thin on specifics, but it could have been a conventional weapon attack or a meta," he finished, brusque.

"So we have no idea what we're dealing with," I said. I slid a palm along the stock of my weapon, taking a deep breath and smelling the gun oil and the other confined scents of the helicopter; Scott's cologne was overpowering as always, as though he had an Abercrombie and Fitch store hidden under his clothes. Zack had toned his down since we had started dating months ago, for which I was still thankful. Kurt, as always, could have stood to go the opposite direction, but I suspected that they had gotten him released from the Medical unit solely for this action. The Directorate's cupboard of resources for a rescue was near-empty if they were sending two newly recovered agents and a suspected traitor on this mission.

The helicopter flew smoothly through the night, the tension inside giving way to an uneasy silence. I looked over at Zack, caught him looking back at me over Jackson, who had taken the seat to my left, and we broke eye contact. Well, I broke eye contact. I wasn't sure what I could say to him other than that I was sorry, and that seemed inadequate given what I had done.

We crossed a river as I looked out the window and saw the half-moon reflected on the water, broken up by the waves running across the surface. We began to descend and I caught sight of cliffs rising out of the water below, hilly terrain on the opposite bank that looked nothing like the smooth fields and woods that surrounded the Directorate. Trees stood out on the edge of the embankments, rough shapes in the dark, shadowed boughs reaching up for us as the pilot took us down a little at a time.

We continued about five minutes past the river to a site where flames were visible in a clearing below us. The helicopter circled, bringing us around for another look before the pilot began a steep descent toward the clearing.

"How many helicopters does the Directorate have, anyway?" Scott asked as we approached the ground, crosswinds causing the whole chopper to buck. I felt the press of my restraints and the chop the closer we got to the ground. Jackson got up and stepped past me, clinging to handles mounted on the ceiling as he slid open the door. I felt one of the wheels touch the ground and Jackson was out, on the ground, sweeping ahead with his weapon. Kurt followed, next out of the chopper while Scott, Zack and the other agent went out the other door.

I unfastened my restraints, realizing I was behind, and stepped off the side of the chopper, nearly wiping out; it was higher off the ground than I thought it would be. I recovered and landed as nimbly as I could given the circumstances, and was on my feet a second later. Helicopter wreckage surrounded us, and trees were visible in all directions, rising up on the sloped ground. We stood in a hilly clearing, underbrush and smaller trees dotting the rocky landscape. The chopper's landing lights were active but not a lot of help for distance vision. A couple small fires remained on the outline of Reed's crashed chopper, but they were dying down.

The area was calm save for the rushing wind around us. My gun was up, the safety off, and I minded my footing as I followed along behind Kurt and Jackson as we wended our way toward the front of the helicopter. A spotlight turned on, giving us a better view of the crash site, casting illumination over the wreckage of the downed helo and forcing me to squint my eyes while they adjusted to the brightness of the spotlight.

The chopper was the older Huey model, smaller than the

Black Hawk we had arrived in. The tail was snapped off, the broken remainder a segment only a couple feet long that was sticking into the air at a forty-five degree angle from the fuselage. The nose was buried, caught in rocks; from where I stood I could look through the door on one side and out the other onto the ground behind it. No bodies were visible in the passenger compartment, the light playing off the dull gray paint job.

"What the hell happened here?" I heard Scott say in my earpiece. I snugged the butt of the gun against my shoulder, felt it push, like the touch of an old friend. It was comforting in the dark. I felt a chill unrelated to temperature; something about being in the woods after midnight, holding a gun, made me tense. I was waiting for something to happen, and I didn't know what. Also, my last experience in the woods hadn't gone so well, and that was in the middle of the day. Night was worse.

"Gonna guess the tail rotor went out," Kurt said, his head swiveling around. "Looks like they spun in."

"What are you, a crash expert?" Scott said, looking in disbelief at the wreckage. "How do you know that?"

"He's right, sir," Jackson said to Scott, more deference in his voice than I would have bothered with. "Looks like they skidded sideways into where it's lodged."

"What does that tell us?" I asked. "If the tail rotor went out, we're not betting it was a mechanical failure, are we?"

"Not unless we're stupid," Zack said under his breath, but his mic picked it up. He cleared his throat when he heard Kurt chuckle and realized what he'd done. "I mean, it seems unlikely." His eyes scanned the site. "Especially since Parks and Reed are missing."

"Looks like the pilots aren't missing..." Scott said, craning his neck to look in the cockpit. "Urk. I take that back; they're missing...some things..."

"Like a head," Zack said, causing me to keep my distance from the wreck. I didn't even bother to make the excuse that I was watching the perimeter; if they'd asked, I would have told them flat out I didn't need to see any more dead bodies for a good long time. "And a neck in the co-pilot's case."

"This can't be from the crash," Scott said, a slight static hiccup marring his words. "There's nothing here that would have caused this kind of damage."

"Oh, you're a forensic pathologist now, are you?" Kurt said. "This from the guy who can't even tell that a helicopter went down sideways."

I listened to them bicker as the clouds blew over the moon, and I shuddered again, a kind of gut-deep nervous tension that was causing my insides to shake, almost like they were clacking together. I hated it, especially because I had nothing to direct it toward. I blinked, felt the fatigue held back by adrenaline from being up when I should have been sleeping, and my eyes watched the woods past our helicopter, which was still sitting about twenty feet away, rotors still spinning, waiting for us. The blades were killing all the ambient noise around us, disrupting any chance I had of gauging any activity. I wanted the pilot to circle and come back, but at the same time I thought that was probably the stupidest idea I could have had; who wanted to send away your escape route when you're alone in the woods at night and something has already knocked one of your helicopters out of the sky?

I saw the movement of the trees as the wind picked up again. It was a cooler wind than at the Directorate, probably because it was blowing west from the river. My skin prickled under my shirt, and my hands tensed inside my gloves, the leather against my flesh giving me no comfort. I kept my finger off the trigger like I'd been taught.

I tasted bitterness in my mouth, and I felt a buzz in my head that I couldn't define, something that was causing all my senses to twitch. "Guys?" I said, and I heard their discussion cease; I had stopped paying attention to it a few minutes earlier. "Something's...wrong here."

"Yeah, our helicopter's down and our people are dead or missing," Scott said, explaining in a tone that told me he thought I was an idiot.

"Beyond that," I said, taking a deep breath and letting it exhale slow. "You think they just sacked the wreckage, killed the pilots and took Parks and Reed with them? Whoever shot down the chopper, I mean?"

"Sounds about right," Kurt said. "Probably burned out afterward."

"Doesn't make sense," I said, and took steps closer to them, avoiding the front of the helicopter, where the pilots were, and looked into the back. One of the things that was bothering me was now clear, something I'd seen without noticing before. "There's no blood in the passenger compartment and the doors are wide open." I clicked my teeth together, trying to find an outlet for my nervous energy. "If it went down, whoever was in the back doesn't look like they were injured, which means—"

"Parks wouldn't have gotten caught easy," Zack finished for me. I felt him next to me, at my shoulder, looking into the compartment for himself. "He could morph into a wolf and outrun almost anyone. And your buddy Reed—"

"He'd ride the wind and blow the hell outta here," Scott said. "Or at least put up a nasty fight; it'd look like a tornado went through the clearing. So, they got out. Where would they go?"

"They'd have to know we'd send help," I said, cautious, and I turned back to the woods, looked at the outline of the darkened trees all around us. "They'd want to hang nearby so they didn't miss rescue."

"Unless they were chased," Kurt said, finally getting into the game. "In which case...what? Outrun and double back?"

"It's what I'd do," Zack said, and I saw Jackson nod. "But that's predicated on losing your pursuers, and hoping they don't get wise to that strategy."

"Then the question is, what kind of pursuers are we dealing with?" I asked, and raised my gun, pointing it at the treeline as I turned in a slow circle. There was movement all around us, but I was unsure whether it was the wind rustling the underbrush, the wash from the helicopter, or something else. "Smart or dumb?"

"Always bet on dumb," Kurt said, but I saw his gun come up to cover the woods that I wasn't.

"I always do with you," I said, tension causing that to pop out. I looked to my right and caught his eyes; he had a half-smile, then shook his head. Hard to define, but I didn't mean it harshly for once, and he didn't take it that way.

"The rotor wash is drowning out everything," Scott said from behind me. "Bigfoot could be sneaking up on us right now and we wouldn't know it."

"I'm not worried about Bigfoot," Zack said. "Since he doesn't exist."

"We trade in mythological creatures and people with beyond human powers," Scott said. "Is it really that hard to believe that Bigfoot exists?"

"Will you idiots cut the chatter about Bigfoot?" A staticky voice broke into our comms, startling me and causing Kurt to jerk, his eyes wide. "Between your idiotic rookie assessments of what happened to our chopper and yours throwing off enough rotor backwash to stir the winds in Eau Claire, I think the things after us are probably well aware of which way we're going."

"Parks?" I asked, cupping my hand to my ear so I could hear him better. "Parks, is that you?"

"Yeah, kid," I heard his gruff voice. "We got two on us, and we're thirty seconds out from your position. Hold your fire."

"You got two what on you?" Zack asked.

There was a pause, and a crackle of static. "That'd be a great question to ask them. Meta of some kind. Nasty. Tore up the pilots while Reed and I were making our escape."

"Wait, did they do that with...like claws or something?" Scott asked. I caught a tenor of fear from him. I understood it, felt a waver of it myself.

"No," Parks' voice came back, winded from running. "Their teeth. They did it with their teeth."

There was a crashing of brush in front of me, undeniable this time, followed by a roar of wind, and I saw Reed whip through the air like he'd taken a long leap assisted by a powerful gust. Parks was a moment behind, the most bizarre thing I'd seen from him yet – his head, mostly human, with the body of a cheetah. He finished the last of his transformation and leapt to his hind legs and ran the last few feet to us, his breath coming in steady gasps.

"I've never been so glad to see you Directorate people as I am now," Reed said, his suit torn in a few places. I saw an open cut on his wrist, blood dripping down his hand. "They're right behind us." I raised my gun and pointed it toward the spot in the woods where they'd come from, but Reed shook his head. "Bullets don't do squat."

I looked to Parks, who nodded. "Emptied a whole clip into one of them and he just shrugged it off. Nasty bastards; never seen anything quite like 'em."

I let the strap take up the weight of my gun and reached down to remove my gloves, quickly, one at a time. "What kind of meta can take bullets and shrug them off? Like Clary?"

Parks shook his head. "No. Something else, not metal at all. Pale skin, red eyes. Nasty teeth."

"Kinda reminded me of Wolfe, in a way, but smaller," Reed said.

"Why are we not getting in the helicopter and leaving?" Jackson said. "We don't need to fight this out right now, do we? We're supposed to retrieve these guys and leave."

"They've got an RPG launcher," Parks said. "You try and

take off now, you'll be back on the ground in two minutes with no extraction."

"Everyone's got rockets nowadays," I said with a sigh. "Whatever happened to settling things mano a mano, with fisticuffs? I like fisticuffs. I just like saying it. Fisticuffs."

"Movement," Kurt announced, and we all closed in tighter. I felt Zack bump into my shoulder, at my back. I exchanged a look with him, and I tried to soften it as much as possible, tried to convey regret, to say, "I'm sorry," with nothing more than my expression. I saw his eyes in the dark, the sorrow in them, and I saw some regret in them as well.

A moment later I heard the movement Kurt had called out; it came through the waist-high shrubs and saplings that surrounded us, rustling the tall grass. I raised my gun and let a three-shot burst rip off at the same time Kurt did. I heard Zack and Jackson firing behind me, and I wondered if the second one was attacking them, or if it was something else entirely.

I fired again as I saw the shadow jump, springing from the grass so fast my eyes could barely track it. It was airborne, in motion, and I shot again, blasting three rounds into it as it soared through the air at face level and hit Kurt. The big man screamed and collapsed under its weight, falling to his back as it came down on him. I heard him cry out again, this time in pain as it struck at him with its head, of which all I could see was black hair.

I moved quickly, taking the two steps toward him, leaning down and seizing it by its throat. I avoided the swipe of a backhand that was led by clawlike fingernails a half inch in length, and I tightened my grasp, my bare hands on its flesh. I ripped it off Kurt, lifting it into the air and over, slamming it into the ground and falling on top of it. At last, with the spotlight shining from the Black Hawk, I got a look at the foe that had stalked Reed and Parks – two of the more fearless men I'd met – and sent them running back to us.

It wore black clothing (I say it, but I think it was a he), and had pallid flesh, almost gray it was so pale. The eyes were indeed red, the irises almost lost in a black pupil that was bigger than a normal human's or meta's, and reminded me of the only time I'd had an eye exam, and what mine had looked like in the mirror after they'd dilated it. Sharp teeth filled the mouth, dozens of them, and it hissed at me as it swiped again. My hands were bare, and I held it at the neck, and it stared at me, those horrid eyes looking into mine. Its hands clamped down on my wrists, and the nails sunk into my arms as those black and red eyes stared back into mine. I couldn't look away, transfixed, horrified.

I pressed the palms of my hands against its throat as it dug its nails into my arms, tearing the skin. I gasped at the pain, waiting, praying the long seconds would go more quickly, would let my power begin to work. Gunfire filled the air around me, and the tingling at my hands, usually so prominent by this point of touch was absent; and I pushed down harder, felt the flesh against my palms, and I squeezed for good measure, but the thing did not even gasp in acknowledgment that I was choking it.

It ran its hands down my forearms, tearing long strips of flesh and drawing a wellspring of blood that flowed down to my hands, making my grip slicker. The creature stopped struggling, eyes wide, and its mouth dropped open, a little smile of horror perched on its lips. It angled its head down as I held on tight, pinning it to the ground. So great was its unconcern at its predicament that it smiled. My touch did nothing, and it extended its tongue and began to lap the blood from my forearm as it flowed from the wounds it had inflicted. Something stirred in the back of my head, fought to warn me, two voices suppressed by drugs and discipline, two people crying out with everything they had, a single word, a warning, and it sprang into my mind full and sent a shot of fear straight through me.

Vampire.

Chapter 12

With the shock of the knowledge, I felt adrenaline course into my veins. I lifted, pulling the vampire to its feet as it jerked in my grasp and tried to sink teeth into my forearm. With a quick turn I threw it, my metahuman strength allowing me to heave him about twenty feet. I watched him twist in the air, his black clothing rippling in the night like a cloud of darkness blotting out the stars. He landed on his feet and was balanced and in motion again a second later, running back toward me, fangs bared and mouth dripping with my blood.

I froze for only a second as someone fired off a burst at him, the flame from the gun barrel lipping, shattering the night with the noise of the shots and destroying my night vision with the barrel flash. It fired again, and I realized it was Jackson, surprisingly calm considering that the vampire was still moving toward us, unerring. The bullets did nothing.

Fire.

The word echoed in my head, another scream of warning from Wolfe and Gavrikov, both of them pressing against the wall between me and them. I regretted for the first time that I had worked so hard to insulate myself from two metas who had centuries and millennia of experience dealing with metahumans, fighting in the very types of conflicts I myself was in on a daily basis. There was nothing I could do about it now but act on the message they worked so hard to get to me.

I swept my head around, looking back to the wreckage of the other helo, to where a few little flames remained in the dry grass. I reached back to where Reed was standing behind me and grabbed his sleeve as he was firing off a tornado-like wind that caught the vampire coming at us and threw him into the air. "Hey!" Reed shouted as I jerked the sleeve of his shredded and mangled suit coat and pulled it loose from him in one good tug, spinning him around like he was caught in his own wind. As he came around I jerked again and freed him from the other sleeve, catching a flash of his irritation as I ran past him toward the wreckage, already balling up the jacket.

I stooped to grab a long, slender piece of metal wreckage about two feet long; it looked like a strut. As I ran I wrapped Reed's coat around it and dipped it into the fire that still burned near the crash, felt the heat and smelled the smoke. The flames took hold and I pulled it out. I held it aloft, my torch, my weapon, and spun back to where the battle was taking place, bullets being sprayed indiscriminately and the vampires having struck down at least two of our people. I could see Reed keeping one of them off of him with some difficulty while Parks had turned into a bear and was battering the other back with Scott's help, a solid stream of water forcing it to be evasive as it ducked and attacked.

"HEY, douchebags!" I shouted. I spun the torch in my hand at my side, felt it whirl like Thor's hammer as I let the icy resolve coat me, erasing that pinch of fear I felt. "Let's have a cook-off. I'll go first." I jumped at the vampire that was coming at Reed – not a little hop, but a twenty-foot leap that would have looked more appropriate on the moon than anywhere near Earth. I came down as he was being buffeted back by Reed's attack. I brought down my torch-club with a solid thud as he tried to block it with a forearm. The physical blow would have been a bone-breaker for a human; as it was I could tell I didn't do anything but tissue dam-age. The impact was solid but bounced off, and I had to use all my strength to hold the weapon in place against the vampire's skin.

While there was no reaction from the blow itself, after a mo-ment of holding the flame against him, I heard a screeching wail that made me wish I had my ear protection on. It was worse than the gunfire by far, higher pitched and not unlike the worst scream I'd ever heard amplified by a factor of fifty. The vampire jerked away from me, falling back to the ground on its side, spinning like a top in a circle and then rolling back to his feet in a bizarre study of motion that probably violated some law of physics. He screamed at me, a hissing squeal that bared his teeth and drew the attention of his partner to me.

I heard the warnings of Scott and Parks at the same time I heard the footfalls. The second vampire, this one blond, did a leap of his own. I turned in time to bring my torch-club around in a swing at waist level and rising. "Batter up," I whispered as I followed through. The club caught the vamp in the midsection and the strength of my swing arrested his momentum and wrapped him around the weapon.

I felt flesh give way to hard metal and meta strength. He flew through the air again, this time up and away from me, arms and legs stretched out limply, trailing the direction of his motion like streamers in the wind behind him. He came to a hard landing about fifteen feet away and I felt a shiver through my arms from the impact, a soreness that I knew my meta healing powers would keep me from feeling tomorrow.

The blond vampire vaulted back to his feet two seconds after landing and let out something between a hiss and a scream, high pitched, that made me cringe and look back to the other. Both of them, now, were dead on target, and the target was me. I took a deep breath as they both twitched, feet anchored in place, looking like they were ready to leap at any moment.

"We need to withdraw," I heard Zack's voice in my ear; he was one of the ones still standing, apparently.

"They've still got an RPG around here somewhere," Parks said. "We get airborne without dealing with it or them, we'll be back down in a worse predicament a few seconds later."

"I'll deal with them," I said, not really feeling the truth of that down to my bones. "Get the wounded to the helo; I'll cover your retreat."

"You're insane," Scott said. "Those things aren't playing; they'll eat your throat out while you're still alive."

"I'll be fine." I kept a wary eye on each as they started to circle around me, not gaining ground, hesitating to spring. "Get moving and I'll be right along."

"What are you gonna do?" I could hear the strain in Zack's voice as he helped Kurt to his feet.

"Not make them sparkle." I tensed and gripped the torch-club even tighter, knowing they'd be striking in tandem.

They broke their holding pattern at the same time, both of them springing into a loping run, scattering dirt with every step. I realized for the first time that they were wearing leather dress shoes to match their black shirts and pants, and I would have laughed if I hadn't been feeling a prickle of concern. They were wicked strong, vicious, more resistant to damage than any meta I'd encountered other than maybe Wolfe or Clary, and they had an appetite for blood – mine, apparently.

They closed the gap and I wondered how I'd deal with both at once when a tornado blew past and flung the raven-haired one into the air again and away from me. I turned to focus on the other, bringing my weapon around and down in an overhand swing. It landed in a perfectly timed blow, hitting the softer neck tissue and the side of the vamp's head, the force of the strike driving him face first into the ground. I didn't feel any pity for this beast and landed another hit to the back of his head as quickly as I could, then another and another before something struck me from behind and I had to roll my way out of the attack as I felt teeth sink into my shoulder.

I hit the ground and jabbed my elbow into the belly of the beast that had gotten me, the black-haired vamp. He didn't let loose, and I felt the teeth dig into my left shoulder. I jerked forward as hard as I could, ripping myself free, losing flesh, muscle and blood in the process. I brought my right hand up and hammered the vamp with three quick blows from the burning club, using the last to jam it into his face, end on, running the flaming cloth hard into his eyes and nose, drawing another hissing scream and several swipes from claws.

I sensed the other coming up on me and turned, bringing the club around in time to catch him across the face. He screamed and I jammed the flaming end into his eyes, and after hearing the same howling noise from him, I ran for the chopper. I could taste blood in my mouth and my left arm was numb. My left shoulder was not; it screamed at me. I saw a few bodies still huddled at the chopper's door, and I realized one of them was Reed, who was climbing inside. Scott was another, though he was already nearly in, pulling something in along with him, something brown and furred – Parks, I realized after a moment, though he was in bear form and bleeding quite a bit. Zack was last, helping to get Parks inside with one hand, while his gun was out and tracking behind me with the other. I couldn't see his face as the spotlight from the front of the helo was nearly blinding me, but I saw him watching, and I heard him when he shouted a warning.

I turned and they were almost on me, the light illuminating both of them, their faces, their fangs. I had burned them, patches of black charring sullying their smooth, pale skin. The light caught the stomach of the blond one I had baseball swung; his belly was laid open from my attack, guts hanging out. It did not seem to affect him as he moved just as effortlessly as the other.

I paused to prepare myself. Raising my weapon and dodging to the side, I hit the blond one with a kick to his open entrails while I swung the club to keep the other back. My kick landed and knocked the blond-haired one to the side while my swing of the club convinced the other to alter his movement to avoid it. He did so successfully and I couldn't follow up, since I was still in the process of catching my balance after the kick.

Blondie dropped to the ground in front of me as I caught my footing. He landed on his back, and before he could scream, as they were so fond of doing, I brought the burning end of the club down and rammed it into his open guts, shoving hard. I wondered if there was any truth to the idea that a stake to the heart would kill them; if so, I assumed a flaming club would do just as well.

He screamed, and it was not a hissing affair, as the others had been. This one was pure, bellowing torment that went up to the heavens as he writhed so hard he bounced a foot off the ground. I shoved him down harder and pushed my weapon into the softness under his ribcage, tearing even louder screams from him. His accomplice hissed at me and drew up for an attack as I withdrew the torch-club, the flame sputtering but still burning, and I waved it in front of me at the other, giving the black-haired vamp pause.

"Succccccubus," he hissed, his black hair and red eyes caught in the light of the helo's spotlight.

"Vaaaaaaampiiiiire," I said, mocking, and I stomped his mewling friend in the face before I took a step away from the prostrated blond fiend. He rocked back and forth slightly, but did not try to get up; had I known a sure way to kill it, I might have taken the chance, but all the methods I could think of were exhausted and I didn't want to take my torch-club away from defending me in order to explore the ins and outs of slaughtering these creatures.

I started circling toward the one still standing; I only needed to take him out of action and we could get airborne and away from these things. "How about you come over here and I'll give you a sweet, tender probing with this?" I waved it in front of my face. "Got an ass? I'll be glad to shove it up there for you. If not, I could always tear you a new one like I did with your pal Spike over there." I waved my club to indicate the blond vampire, still writhing on the ground.

He hissed at me, but didn't reply other than to keep up with the circling. He maintained a distance of about twenty feet from me, but now he was heading more toward the chopper and the doors. I could see everyone was aboard now, and I heard the rotors spinning up, the speed of their rotation increasing as it readied for takeoff. He sashayed toward the entry and I began to fear what he might try when he reached the door. I took two steps forward and, mindful of the rotor above, lunged at him, keeping my head down and swinging the club in an arc in front of me.

The black-haired vamp dodged and halted by the door. I came at him again, this time drawing the torch behind me, giving him an opening. I saw his red eyes flash and I slowed myself, trying to entice him to make a move. He went for it, leaping at me, keeping low enough to dodge the rotor, and he caught me as I brought the weapon back around, grasping onto my arm and sinking his nails into it. I felt pain that I dismissed and began a full spin with him hanging onto my arm and shoulder. He was off-balance, and I ripped him from the ground, whipping him around as if he were a club I were swinging.

I brought him around, using my strength and some momentum to sweep him through the air. I let loose of him after bringing him in a full circle. I felt his claws tear flesh as his momentum carried him about ten feet back, where he spun perfectly to allow the tail rotor to catch him in the belly. The shriek of metal buzzing was like a blender hitting something it wasn't supposed to and a grinding noise ensued as he was flung away, back to the ground after a sharp bounce against the main rotor. He landed a few feet from me, a bloody mess, his guts in worse state than the blond one, who was starting to push to his feet, albeit slowly.

I took a step toward him. "Okay, Angel, let's see how tough you really are to kill." I felt a hand grab hold of me from behind.

I raised my club and started to swing but stopped; it was

Zack. "Let's go," he said, and pointed to the blond vamp, who was starting to pick himself up off the ground, still a horrific mess, but almost mobile. "You could tangle with them all night and not kill them." He looked me in the eyes, and I read the urgency in them. "Come on." I tossed the club at the blond-haired one, hearing the satisfying sound of the metal hit him in the face as I let Zack lead me, his hand taking care to grasp me by the shredded cloth of my shirt that still clung to my arm as he guided me into the cabin of the Black Hawk.

"Problem with the tail rotor," I heard the pilot say as we got inside. "Engine's gonna have some issues after being hit like that."

"I'll keep it spinning," Reed said, stepping up to the door and sticking a hand out. I watched a vortex form around the laboring tail rotor, which appeared to be rotating on a strange off-axis, wobbling. "Just get us in the air."

"All right," I heard the pilot shout back, and we started to rise.

I saw sweat beads pop out on Reed's forehead. "You might want to sit down," he said. "I can't guarantee the quality of the ride we're about to experience."

I let Zack lead me to my seat and help strap me in. I looked down at my arms, which were slick with blood, dripping to my hands. I held them up and looked at my palms, covered and slick, and marveled that I had been able to keep a grip on the club. They were shaking now, and numb, but what little I could feel hurt a lot. Zack fastened me into my seat without saying anything, but his eyes said enough for an entire conversation. He buckled me in and sat down, with only a glance at Reed, then me, before he took his own seat. We were rattling, but in the air now, shaking with the currents that Reed was summoning to keep us aloft and from spinning out. But me – I was shaking for an entirely different reason, both inside and out, as we swirled through the hot summer night and back home.

Chapter 13

We set down a few minutes later at the Directorate after what could only be described as an uneven ride. We bumped on the final touchdown and I heard the engines throttle down, the rotors coming to a slow stop as several loud, clunking noises came from the rear of the craft. Smoke had been belching out of it the whole way home, but Reed's wind had blown that clear of us and we only knew about it because of the pilot's occasional warnings.

I breathed a little sigh of relief when I felt that last shudder of the aircraft's weight being taken up by the earth, and I closed my eyes for a beat before I opened them to look out the door. Ariadne was waiting, as was Dr. Perugini, Dr. Zollers, a couple of people I'd seen Perugini use before as orderlies, and my most favoritest person in the world, Michael Mormont. Eve lurked behind them, looking around as if searching for the ambush that was sure to fall on us at any moment. A couple of agents were visible in the distance, but I couldn't see their faces from where they stood outside the field of spotlights that illuminated the helicopter pad.

The orderlies rushed up along with Perugini, and Kurt went onto a gurney, swearing as they moved him. He'd gotten cut up pretty well by the vamps, but not as bad as the agent whose name I hadn't known – he was dead. Total redshirt. Parks got off a minute later with help from Scott, but he had a hobble as he walked, following in the wake of Perugini and the orderlies.

I felt a tug and realized Zack was undoing my safety harness. "Hey," he said, taking care to move it from around my shoulders. "We're here."

"Okay," I said as I shrugged out of the other side. I stepped toward the door and onto the concrete below, as Ariadne waited for me with Zollers and Mormont. Zack followed, and as I stepped out I noticed Reed leaning heavily against the open door, his head back against the hard metal and his eyes closed.

"What happened?" Ariadne asked as she looked at my bloody hands and arms. "What did you run across?"

"Vampires," I said, and let out the breath I hadn't even realized I'd been holding. "Nobody told me there were vampires."

Ariadne stared at me blankly. "I...I didn't know there WERE vampires. Are you sure that's what you saw?"

I held my arms up and she balked at the sight of the puncture wounds, the blood. "Pretty sure."

"Are you all right?" Zollers asked me, his eyes rimmed with concern.

"I'll heal," I said. "But I would like to know why Omega has vampires and we didn't know about it."

"Add it to the list of things Omega has sucker-punched us with," Zack said. "It's getting to be a pretty long one."

"I knew they had vampires," Reed said at last, and his every word sounded like it was being dragged from his lips with a winch and chain. "I didn't know that's what they looked like, or that they were even in the U.S., but I knew they had them. Sorry; I guess I should have figured they'd have brought in the blood hunters."

"Blood hunters?" This from Mormont, who I can only assume took affront at the vamps stealing his hard-earned title.

Reed opened his eyes and tried to push himself off the door to a standing position, but after wavering and looking like he would fall, let himself lean back onto the door and slid down to the ground, eyes shut again. I would have helped him, but frankly I doubted my ability to stand up straight without him weighing me down, let alone with. "That's what they are. They hunt blood, like a bloodhound. They get a rush from consuming it, like a natural high. They can smell it, seek it out."

"They seemed pretty close to invulnerable to me," Zack said. "Like the legends, I guess. But do you really need a stake to kill them, or sunlight?"

"Myth, legend...you know how it goes," Reed said from the ground. "Exaggerated. They have a hell of a bone structure, though, stronger than a normal person's or even a normal meta's, so it's really damned hard to land a damaging blow on them. They don't feel pain like us, can ignore it and keep coming. You saw – that one had a belly open to the air and he was about to come at Sienna again. They're nocturnal, can see in the dark like it's day, have nearly unbreakable bones, heal super fast – faster than even most metas – and all that makes them hard to kill and terrific hunters when you're looking to track someone down." He took another breath. "Never had seen one of them until tonight, and I wouldn't have recognized them for what they were if Sienna hadn't called it out."

Heads swiveled to me, Ariadne's and Mormont's foremost among them. Zollers watched me too, but coolly, like it was no big deal. "How did you know what they were?" Mormont found the words to ask first.

"Voices in my head," I said, drawing a surprised look from Ariadne, but not Zollers. Mormont's eyes narrowed. "They practically had to scream to get me to hear," I went on, "but the message got through."

"I hate to interrupt this lovely conversation," Zollers said, still heavy with sincerity and concern, "but could we adjourn to the medical unit? I'd like to insure that Sienna gets bandaged up."

"What, these?" I held my forearms up, and watched a small shower of droplets hit the concrete below, looking almost like water droplets in the heavy floodlights. I took a deep breath through the nose and could have sworn I smelled the iron in the blood, which had mostly clotted by now. "No big deal."

"All the same," Zollers said, "let me bandage you up." He

held out an arm in invitation, sweeping it to indicate that we should walk toward the headquarters building.

"Why?" I asked, almost uncaring. "It'll heal by tomorrow anyway."

"Consider it a courtesy to those of us who don't like to see you bleed." His eyes were warm, and I felt my resistance and uncaring fade, and I started along meekly.

"Don't mind me," Reed said from behind me, still seated by the helicopter. "I'm just going to sleep here."

"Zack," Ariadne said, "please help Mr. Treston to his room, will you?" She looked down to Reed. "We'll talk about your conversation with your headquarters tomorrow, unless you have anything desperately urgent to tell us now?"

I watched Reed open an eye. "Nothing catastrophically revealing – I'm allowed to help you. And one other thing – you've got a traitor in your organization."

"Well yeah," I said after a minute, "we've known that since Andromeda told us before, remember?"

"Yeah," Reed said with a shake of his head. "Some detail, though – they're highly placed. Our sources inside Omega say your traitor has access to nearly everything." He blinked. "Which might explain to you how they managed to set a trap to ambush my helicopter. They even knew the flight path we were taking and put those vamps in our way with a guided missile to take me down."

"But why?" Ariadne asked. "Why bother, when you didn't really have anything to tell us?"

"Because," Reed said with a tired smile, "the worst thing for Omega would be the joining of their worst enemy – us – with the most powerful meta force in North America. It's the unholy union of old-world knowledge of metahumans with the new school of technology and science." He shrugged, but it was a weary sort of sad one. "Looks like they mean to wipe you out in the next few moves, and I think they worry we might be an impediment to that."

"Why?" Ariadne said, and she actually stooped to look at Reed when she said it. "We've had no run-ins with them, really." She paused, gave it a thought, and went on. "Other than over—"

"Her," Reed said with a nod to me.

"I'm sorry, what?" I blinked and looked around at the circle of faces that had turned to me. "Me? You told me before they were after my mom, that they were using me to get to her."

"Sienna's why they're attacking you," Reed said. "All along they've been after her, since the day they sent Wolfe to retrieve her. They've got a mean-on for her for some reason, and no one knows what it is. And I'm starting to think it might not have anything to do with her mother at all; they've been more or less ignoring Sierra, after all."

"What about you?" I asked. "You've been after me nearly as long."

"Because Wolfe was after you," Reed said, eyes on mine, but a veil over his, where I couldn't quite tell what he was thinking but could see there was something more to it. "I got the word he was on your trail and I tried to get there first." He looked to Ariadne, who was still next to me. "What about you? How did you know to go for her?"

Ariadne hesitated. "I don't know," she said, and I remembered long ago when I'd had a conversation with her in a confining room when I'd first awakened at the Directorate. "The Director handed me her address and flagged her to be brought in immediately, highest priority—"

"Interesting," I said, a little smug. "That's not what you told me when you brought me in."

"And if you'd asked the Director," she said, flicking a cool look back at me that contained more than a grain of discomfort at having to admit her lie, "do you think he would have told you if he didn't want to?"

"I guess we'll find out," I said solemnly. "Where is he?"

"Texas," Ariadne said as Zack helped Reed to his feet. "He's at our campus down there trying to help them get back on their feet." She looked at Reed almost apologetically, and he raised an eyebrow as he leaned most of his weight on Zack. "Metaphorically speaking. You're more than welcome to ask him when he gets back, but it could be several days, as he's somewhat busy helping them deal with the massacre of almost ninety percent of their agents by Omega."

"I'm sorry," I said, turning to Reed, who was already beginning to hobble away with Zack's help. He didn't turn back to me, though Zack turned to look. "Are you suggesting that this whole war with Omega is because of...of..." I floundered for a moment. "Because of me?"

Zack stopped, and after a moment Reed turned with him, a slow circle Zack walked while keeping Reed in roughly the same place. "I'm sorry," Reed said. "I didn't mean to suggest it." I took a breath until he spoke again and it all came out in a gasp. "I meant to say it flat out." His eyes were laden with sympathy for me. "You are the flashpoint, the reason that Omega is at war with the Directorate. It's because they wanted you and were thwarted twice, losing two of their most powerful operatives. That's not the sort of threat to their influence and reputation in the meta world that they could tolerate." He blinked. "So they came at your support mechanism, seeing weakness there." He smiled again. "After all, with the Directorate gone, who's going to protect you?"

Chapter 14

I let Dr. Zollers lead me off to the medical unit without protest, let him gesture me over to a bed where I sat, staring ahead, trying not to think about everything going on but failing miserably. He came back in a moment with three layers of latex gloves on, some bandages in hand, and disinfectant. "This will probably sting some," he cautioned as he rolled a stool up to sit in front of me.

"Worse than when my arms got raked apart to begin with?" I asked with a dull smile.

"Probably not," he conceded as he started to examine them. "I doubt this is enough of a layer of protection from your powers—" he held up a gloved hand – "so I'm going to minimize flesh contact." He extended a swab after dabbing it in the disinfectant. "This is more of a precaution. I know you'll heal on your own."

"Then why are you doing this?" I held my hand out and he ran the swab down one of the gouges in my flesh. "Why bother?"

He seemed to think about it for a moment as he worked, staring intently at what he was doing. "Because it feels better than doing nothing."

"But it's pointless," I said. "Won't change a thing."

"Wrong," he said. "I told you, it feels better than doing nothing; ergo, it changes how I feel. That's not nothing."

"It's not important how we feel," I said. "It's important what we do."

He raised an eyebrow at me and stopped his work on my arm. "That is possibly the most incorrect thing I've ever heard, and dangerous to boot. Ever tried to ignore overwhelming feelings for too long? How do you think it turns out? Well?"

"I don't know. Probably not."

"Yeah," he said, looking back down with the swab in motion, stinging me. "Probably not. Human emotions are like the most fearsome lions when aroused, and yet as easily torn through as a paper tiger at times. Ignore them at your peril."

"My feelings lead me in stupid directions," I said, staring at the metal wall, trying not to look at Kurt a few beds away or the body in the distance of the unnamed agent who was covered by a white sheet that had started to tint red with blood. "I don't like going in stupid directions. The heart betrays you."

Zollers didn't answer for a minute and I wondered if he had heard me but decided not to argue. "Sometimes."

I chuckled, but it wasn't with any real feeling. "That's what you've got to make me feel better? I thought you'd try and talk me out of it."

"Try and talk you out of thinking that the human heart is capable of making some dumb decisions?" Zollers looked up at me. "Far be it from me to try and convince you of that. It absolutely is capable of making stupid decisions. But they're not always wrong ones, even if they are inconvenient." He took a bandage and ran medical tape along the sides before wrapping it over my arm and running a finger along the tape. "Take you, for instance – you might be a little conflicted right now—"

"I might be," I said coolly, interrupting him.

"But I think your heart is in the right place," he said. "For example, your mother is in direct conflict with the organization you work for. Now, your mother and you have a history, to put it in mildest terms. Still, there's a connection, and someone who didn't know better might think you could feel guilty for not helping her."

"That'd be a stupid way to feel," I said, the crimson burning my cheeks. "Especially since she hasn't asked for my help and seems to want to be around anyone but me, if possible."

"Oh my," he said and stopped again, this time looking me in

the eye. "You're jealous of Kat?" He raised an eyebrow again. "What? You didn't get enough of being locked up by her the first time around? You feeling a little homesick?"

"Oh shut up," I said mildly, even though I was annoyed. "No, I'm not...homesick or eager to get locked away again. I just...I don't know."

"You wish your mother had cared enough to want to take you with her." He said it certain, and that certainty pissed me off. "You don't know, she might—"

"She might have a lot of things," I snapped at him. "She might have wanted to, she might not have been able to, she might have been playing a dangerous game that she didn't want me involved in – I've thought of all of them. But you know the conclusion I've come to after all that? She didn't want me with her for the same reason she disappeared for months and months. She came here, to the campus, and didn't want me to go with her when she left. She ran into me beaten, bloodied, near dead and she didn't want me with her then, either. I think it's time to face facts," I said with a cold smile. "She's finished being my mother. Nothing left to do, nothing left to be said between us." I felt a cold satisfaction at the words. "She cast me out, said, 'best of luck,' and that's it. She's done with me." I held my head up. "And me? I'm done with her, too." I brought my hands down and felt a lump in my pocket – the watch, the one that came with the note that said my father had wanted me to have it. I moved my hand away.

Zollers started to say something but I caught a flinch from him as though he'd been struck, a cringe that hinted at something bad. The door to the medical unit slid open a moment later and Michael Mormont appeared, a calm smile on his face, Eve Kappler a few steps behind him. He looked around the unit, past where Dr. Perugini was working on Kurt, and over to Zollers and me. Within a second of locking eyes with me he came my way and I felt the dread in my stomach rise unexplainably. Well, I might be able to explain it.

"Well, well," Mormont said as Zollers rose from the stool after sliding his finger along the edge of a bandage, pressing it to my flesh. "Feeling any better?"

"Not much," I said, holding up my unbandaged arm. "Why? Do you care?"

"Not really," he said with a little shrug. "I need you to come with me, back to headquarters."

"We're in the middle of this right now," Zollers said, pointing to my still-bloody right arm. "Can it wait just a few minutes?"

"Hardly." He nodded at Eve, who looked at me in her usual inscrutable solemnity and walked behind the bed I was sitting on. I turned to track her, but Mormont spoke and drew my attention back to him. "Ariadne wants you at HQ."

I exchanged a look with Zollers, whose eyes held something I couldn't understand. "Fine," I said, and stood up, letting my feet fall the half foot to the floor from the bed. "But I—" I stopped as I felt hands behind mine, and felt something hard and metal close onto my wrist, like when Clary had clamped his hands down on them. The pain seared on my open cuts and I swore. "What the f—"

"Handcuffs," Mormont said with a smile. "They're something new, designed to hold even a top-of-the-scale meta like you."

"Is this really necessary?" Zollers asked with a tired look, as though he already knew the answer.

"Yeah, it's necessary," Mormont said, and his hand went into his pocket. "You know what this is?" His hand came out with something small between his thumb and forefinger, something small enough I couldn't really see it from a few feet away.

"Yeah," I said snottily, "it's your d—" A hard blow to the back of the head dropped me to the ground as Eve drove an elbow into me that caused a flash in front of my eyes.

"I shouldn't be surprised you'd go to the lowest common denominator when it comes to defiant answers," Mormont said as I stared at his shoe, my cheek on the floor, blood in my mouth. I felt Eve's hands seize me around my sleeve as she dragged me back to my feet.

"Manners," Eve said in that stiff German accent of hers. I restrained myself from spitting blood in her face in response, instead let it drip, felt it go down my chin.

"This is ridiculous," Zollers said, anger rising. "I'll be reporting your conduct – both of you – to the Director."

"He won't do anything," Mormont said, and his hand came up again. "As I was saying – this is a listening device. Found it in Ariadne's office. Small scale, short range, so whoever was listening to it was right here on campus."

"Congratulations," Zollers said dryly. "There are hundreds of people on campus. Why are you harassing this one?"

"Very simple, Doc," Mormont said with a smirk. "Because when I searched her room a few minutes ago – and yes, she was the first person I suspected, but for other reasons – what do you think I found?" The smirk grew wider but Zollers failed to react. "If you guessed the matching set for listening into this, you'd be right. Just turned it on—" he pulled a little black box from his suit's other pocket, something that looked a little bigger than an MP3 player, complete with a headset – "and suddenly I hear the world's worst case of screeching feedback." He held them both up in front of him, the microphone and the bug. "Still want to defend her?"

"Absolutely," Zollers said, clenching his teeth. "You've got not one speck of evidence that these belong to her."

Mormont shrugged. "I found 'em in her room, Doc."

"I really oughta start locking my door," I said through a rapidly swelling lip.

"I wouldn't worry about that," Mormont said, grinning at me. "You're coming back to headquarters to answer some questions.

And regardless of how that goes, Ariadne has declared you a person of suspicion." He took a breath through his nose as though he were savoring the moment. "Couldn't have said it better myself, because I've got some suspicions about you." His smile broadened. "So you don't have to worry about locking your door for a while, because where you're going, it'll be locked...pretty much all the time."

Chapter 15

The air was thick in the box. The cool damp of the basement faded as the air had become warm and stuffy inside. I could see the light coming in from the seam around the door of the box, streaming in from outside the basement's painted windows. Of course, I couldn't see them, but since Mom had turned off the basement light, I knew it was daytime now. I had been in the box for over eighteen hours by my reckoning.

My back and legs were stiff. I was sitting, my knees bent in front of me, crammed sideways into the box and taking up every inch of space. The pressure of the metal against my back and my legs was tight because of how little room I had. I felt numb. I was sitting in my own filth and had been since yesterday. The smell would have been unbearable but I had been exposed to it for so long that now it was just another constant, like the tapping of the pipes overhead in the basement as water ran through them, or the thrumming of the air conditioner unit outside as it started to run every hour or so.

I leaned my head against the metal side, and smacked my lips together. I hadn't had a drink of water since I was locked in, which meant I was due to get out soon, I hoped. Mom never left me without water for more than a day. I felt weak and my stomach roared with desire for food. I didn't even care if I showered, I was so hungry and thirsty. I had sobbed myself to sleep in the darkness and I woke up frequently throughout the night, the discomfort to my neck and back causing me to awaken at unusual times. Once, I had a fit, the claustrophobia pressing in on me when it was totally dark, and I slammed my hand against the metal until it bled, but afterward I had broken down and started crying, and fell back asleep for a little while. When I woke up, I was calm again.

I heard something outside, faint tapping. I listened and realized it was footsteps on the stairs. I heard them leave the wood steps and pad onto the foam mats that covered the basement floor where we practiced martial arts. They halted outside the box and I held my breath, daring to hope it was over. I heard a screech of metal as the little slot above me opened, and I struggled to my feet, willing my legs to work after being crammed in a desperately uncomfortable position overnight.

The light streamed in from the aperture. I looked out and squinted my eyes shut. The light was so bright, it hurt my eyes like someone was sticking their fingers into them. I opened them slowly, little by little, over ten seconds and looked out. A shadowed face stood a few feet away, and I could see the disappointment even through my squint. I smacked my dry lips together, hoping for some moisture. "Hi, Mom," I said.

She didn't answer me at first, and I saw her hand reach toward me, the light catching something she was holding, glinting and shining through it. She brought it up to the window – a water bottle, filled. I reached up, desperate, banged my elbow on the side of the box, sending a shock of pain to my fingers, but I didn't care. I grasped at it, pulled it from her and heard the satisfying crack as I broke the seal and twisted, my hands shaking as I did so. I brought it up to my lips and felt the cool water pour over them, cracked, and felt it caress my tongue, coating my mouth. It reminded me of a plant we'd had in the kitchen years ago, in a red clay pot – the dirt had dried out after a few days and when I poured water into it after remembering that I had to water it, it stayed on top of the dry soil for a few minutes before soaking in. My mouth felt that way, like the water was sitting in it, waiting to absorb through the tissue and re-hydrate everything, like that dry soil.

I swallowed and felt the cool water running down my throat, and chugged it, drinking hungrily. My stomach roared as the liquid fell into it, a pitiful sacrifice and not at all what the rulers of my belly wanted, but it would have to do for now. My skin was sticky everywhere, and my clothes clung to me. As the water cleansed that awful taste of bitterness off my tongue, it was replaced by the seeping smell of the box, of me.

"Have you had enough?" Mom leaned forward and rested her hand on the opening of the slit through which she passed me the water. I saw her eyes, intense, staring in at me.

I remained silent as I took the last drink. I felt sick in my stomach, pain and cramping from drinking it too fast after not having anything for so long. "Yes," I whispered with a slight spray of spittle as I pulled the plastic ring of the bottle away from my mouth. "Yes."

"I don't expect we're going to have any more problems with you doing your chores, then?" There was a tone of patient expectation, but it was harsh, and cold.

I felt resentment stir, tempting me to say something I would regret. "No," I answered after a beat, and only a beat.

"All right," she said, and I heard the pin slide out, unlocking the box. She stepped back and the door swung open from its own weight, on a slow arc. I took two steps and fell onto the mat, felt my knees give out and send my face against the canvas, where it rested. My legs stretched out and I enjoyed the feeling of open space, unfettered, uncramped, and I let myself rest, face down.

"When you're done, get upstairs and shower, then fix yourself some breakfast." I turned my face to look up at her from where I lay. She stared down at me, her arms still crossed. "I'm going to work. When I come home tonight, my bathroom had better be clean." I still felt a dryness in my mouth, and I looked up at her.

"Do you hear me?" she asked, and I shied my eyes away from her and nodded. "I can't hear you nod your head," she said, and I stared down at my sweatpants, stained from my hours trapped in the metal case behind me. "Answer me," she said with rising urgency.

"Yes," I said, my voice cracking. "I'll clean it up."

"Good." She took a step away. I still didn't look at her, but stayed on the mat, pressing my face against it, smelling the sweat of all our efforts, our workouts, on it, and loving that smell more than the overpowering one that radiated everywhere in the basement, from the box, from that hell. "Now clean yourself up. Only someone who's totally pathetic would just lay around on the floor all day. Get up." I heard her feet recede onto the stairs, heard them click against the wood steps, one by one, and I knew she wasn't looking at me anymore.

I heard her feet overhead, heard her walk to the front door and open it, heard the tell-tale beep of the alarm, then heard the door shut again. I sighed, and I continued to lay there, my face pressed against the mat, and I didn't get up for several more hours.

Chapter 16

Now

I awoke on a narrow cot, my eyelids fluttering as I heard something. The room I was in was small, about ten feet by ten feet, an army-style cot in the middle of it and not much else for decor. The walls were bare and set in small segments, carved squares from floor to ceiling, which was a good ways above my head. It was the room I'd woken up in after arriving at the Directorate for the first time, or at least one identical. There was a single glass pane on the wall opposite me, and I waved humorlessly at it with a big, fake, smarmy smile as I sat up and felt my feet touch the floor. The floor was dry, and squeaked as I rubbed my sock against it.

I shook the cobwebs out of my brain and rubbed my eyes. The lights turned on as I moved, either because they were set to motion sensors or because someone watching on the other side of the mirrored glass decided to grace me with illumination. I blinked as the lights flickered on overhead, the sterile fluorescence painting the scene in even starker black and white detail, the gray of the squared walls a depressing spectacle.

"I have to go to the bathroom," I said aloud, feeling the pressure on my bladder that came after awakening. I waited, and didn't hear anything for a few minutes. I stared at the walls, trying to remember which set of squares concealed the door; it was hidden into the ornamentation of the wall, which was both annoying and probably very practical for when they kept prisoners. Disorientation makes it harder to escape, after all.

I heard the faint hum of the overhead lights and nothing else save for my steady breathing, which I had been attuned to since I woke up. There was no real smell in the air; it was a room well ventilated and there was not even a scent of the air conditioner at work, or of food (though I was hungry and thought I might be imagining the smell of pancakes), and the feel of my weight on the cot was infinite, enough to make me not bother even standing up. What was the point, anyway?

I heard a series of clicks come from the wall to my left and I turned my head as the door opened, appearing as if by magic from the lined squares on the wall. A familiar face stepped inside, along with a familiar body – Zack's dirty blond hair at the top of his lean frame, his face grimmer than I remembered it being last week, when we were still dating. "Come on," he said with a jerk of his head toward the exit.

I stood and walked over to him, my feet feeling the firmness of the tiled floor which seemed metal, it was so cool and steely. He moved back from the door to let me pass and once I was in the colorless hall, he gestured which way to go, and that I should walk in front of him. I didn't want to break the silence (and I didn't really have anything to say to him, anyway), so I just went along. He led me to the bathroom and left me alone for a few minutes while I showered. There were fresh clothes laid out for me and I put them on, not bothering to dry my hair since there was no hair dryer. I didn't have anywhere to be, anyway, and the damp coolness of it brushing against my neck was a pleasant enough sensation.

Once done, I took a syringe out of the small leather case, along with the vial of clear liquid that was waiting. I tapped my arm until I found a vein and slipped the needle in, not even wincing at the pinching sensation. I was getting pretty good at this. I put my gloves back on when I was done, ignoring the little drop of blood that sprang up; it would be gone in a minute.

I pulled on the University of Minnesota sweatshirt that was

waiting for me. It had a familiar aroma, and I put my nose up to it – it smelled like Zack. The jeans were all me, though, and I put them on along with socks and walked out of the bathroom with my wet hair still against my neck. He was looking down as I came out of the bathroom. I could have knocked him senseless by the time he had brought his head up, but why? Where else would I go? What would I do?

He followed me back to my little square room and I went inside wordlessly, turning to look at him as he stood at the entrance, staring in at me, face inscrutable. "How long until I can get out again?" I asked. "Because if you're going to keep me under wraps for a good long while, you might consider transferring me to Arizona—"

"You're not going to Arizona," he said, and I watched his brow crease and turn down.

"You sound pretty sure of that," I said, and I realized I sounded as sad as he did.

"You didn't betray the Directorate," he said, and he looked away for a moment before his gaze came back to my eyes. "I'd stake everything on it."

"Nice to know somebody believes." I felt that burning at my eyes again. "Even after—"

"Don't."

I nodded. "Okay."

He took a step back and his hand caught the door, ready to close it, but he hesitated. "Why?"

I stared at him, trying to pretend I didn't know what he meant. "Why what?"

"You know," he said.

I shrugged and tried to play it off. "I don't. Why what? Why am I in here? Great question. I'd like to know the answer myself—"

"Why did you break up with me, then almost sleep with another guy?" I blinked as he said it, felt the gut punch of emotion that came with it, and resisted it with everything I had, tried to pretend there were little pipes that ran through my whole body that carried emotion. I could feel them twisting my stomach and I tried to pretend I could just shunt them away, away from my heart, from my eyes.

I let the question hang in the air between us as though it were a bomb, ready to explode, and all it would take is the lightest touch from me to set it off. I didn't look at him, but took a few steps back to where I knew the cot was, and I lowered myself down on it. "I don't know," I said, more out of reflex than truth. I was stalling, unsure of what to say or how to say it.

"That's it?" He shook his head and started to shut the door.

"Wait," I said, quiet. "Because there's no future for us." I looked up at him and saw eyes filled with pain. "None. With me, you'd always live half a life, and you didn't have the guts to pull the trigger, so I did."

"Oh, you're so noble," he said, words dripping with sarcasm. "Thank you for thinking of me when you did that. When you started to sleep with the other guy, were you thinking of me then, too?"

"Yes," I said. "I was thinking of you then. I was wishing it was you."

The little head of steam, of righteous indignation, I could see building in him just deflated. His wounded look crumpled into something else, his face fell, the anger gone. "Why did you do it?"

"I don't know," I answered honestly. "I was a little drunk. Not too gone, but just…there. And he touched me, and I realized I could touch, and I just…" I shook my head. "I just did. It was stupid, and it was reckless, and it was unlike everything I knew I should do, and I did it anyway. Because I wanted to." I blinked at him. "Because I couldn't with you." I didn't put an ounce of blame into the last bit, just let it ooze with regret and pain, and I saw him take another step back, stare at me from the door for another minute without saying anything, until he finally closed it. The clunking noise it made as the lock slid back into place was the last noise I heard for several hours afterward.

The look on his face stayed with me long, long after that.

Chapter 17

The lights stayed on, even when I lay for a while on my cot, staring up at the ceiling, composed of (what else?) squares of ceiling tile. They were one-foot segments, I figured out at last, ten in a row on each side, a hundred in total, and for some reason that number appealed to me, and I found it oddly comforting. I counted the walls and realized they were in the same configuration, then looked at the floor and realized that though the tile there was different than the steel walls, it was the same size. I was surrounded by six hundred equal-sized squares, six hundred little squares that made up the big cube that I was in.

One big box.

I spent a little time examining the watch that I still had in my pocket. I didn't know if it was a mark of trust that they hadn't bothered to search me, or if they were just that lax in their security. I had no idea if it was set to the proper time, but I watched the second hand tick away, the finest entertainment I had with me. No one burst into the room and took it from me, and I was sure they were watching, so I chalked it up to them not caring I had it.

When the door opened again, the noise of the lock sliding cued me to look for it. I didn't bother getting up, though. I hadn't eaten yet today, which was a mark in nobody's favor, but I hadn't asked, either. I was a little thirsty, but again, I hadn't asked for anything to drink because it hadn't gotten urgent yet. Frankly, this was nothing. I had plenty of space to move, if I wanted to. I didn't want to.

The door opened and Ariadne came in with a tray, cafeteria food resting on it. I saw meatloaf, which I hate, but I was past the point of being picky. I stared at Ariadne when she came in; she stared back at me. "I brought you lunch," she said at last, reluctant. Her heels clicked on the tile like a hammer hitting concrete, each step at odds with her manner, which was mousy and hesitant.

"I didn't know we'd moved past breakfast yet, since I didn't get any."

"I'm sorry," she said, and brought the tray over to me, extending it with one hand. It was light, I could tell, a styofoam plate on a brown tray, with a little plastic spork and a couple cartons of milk, like I was a kid. The meatloaf itself had some red ketchup on it, the only point of color on the tray, and it reminded me of my hands after my fight with the vampires. Or after Andromeda died.

"I asked Zack if you were going to ship me to Arizona," I said, breaking the spork out of the little plastic bag that it was sealed in. I balanced the tray on my knees and Ariadne stood above me as I took my first bite, taking care to get plenty of ketchup to cover the taste of the meatloaf itself.

"No," she said. "I wouldn't even be holding you like this if not for the fact that finding the bug in your room is the last in a long line of circumstantial evidence—"

"My circumstances suck." I took another bite and chewed as I thought about that.

"But it could all be wild coincidence," she said, as she lowered herself to sit next to me. She didn't look at me as she did so, and I cast her a sidelong glance that it was probably better she didn't catch full-on. "I'm aware that nothing we've got is really proof; not the kind I'd like before accusing a long-standing trainee of betraying us—"

"Why?" I said with a shrug. "I think it's obvious at this point that my mother is playing some sort of game here. If she was willing to keep me locked in a house for over a decade, is it really out of the realm of possibility that she'd try and stick me undercover here for six months to pull off whatever it is she's up to?" I shrugged, balancing the tray. "I don't think that's farfetched."

Ariadne looked over at me. "I don't think it's out of the realm of possibility for her. I think it would be completely out of character for *you*."

I froze, spork halfway to my mouth, and just held it there. I didn't want to look at her. I forced the bite into my mouth and chewed it slowly, swallowing it with extreme difficulty. "What are you going to do with me?"

She seemed to crumple under forces that were not visible to the eye. "I don't know. Wait for the Director to return from Texas and make the decision for me."

I could have made some crack about the pressure of leadership on her, or how she might not be up to it, but I couldn't think of one, and I didn't really want to anyway. "I don't want to be in here anymore," I said, and meant it. I sat the tray on the ground and looked at the walls, and the room seemed smaller than ten by ten by ten now, much smaller.

"I know," she said.

"Know, but don't care?" My voice was shot through with more than a little 'don't care' as well.

"I wouldn't say that." She leaned forward, placed her hands on her knees and then stood up. "I've got J.J. in a cell, too, which isn't making me feel any better. And Kurt."

My eyebrow spiked in a raise. "Kurt?"

She cocked her head. "They left him alive when they ambushed you; that's more than a little suspicious since they tried to kill the rest of you. I'd put your friend Reed in a cell too, but I can't really afford to alienate Alpha since they seem to be the only allies we've got."

Words broke through the wall around my head. "Why do you have J.J. in a cell?"

"Because he, you, Reed, Parks and the pilots were the only ones that knew about Reed's little excursion home to call his bosses," she said, looking down at me, her shock of red hair the only color in the room.

"But I thought your office was bugged," I said with a shake of my head. Wasn't that the reason I was here?

"It appeared to be," she said. "But my office gets swept regularly for listening devices, and this one just happened to be there right after our conversation. It could have been placed by any number of people, but the timing is just strange. The last sweep of my office was at midday. I have a list of appointments during that time, a half-dozen people, and Mormont is interviewing every one of them, too." She shrugged. "I'm following Mormont's recommendations on this until the Director has a chance to weigh in. It's clear that the chopper flight was betrayed to Omega to give them a chance to shoot it down and kill Reed, cutting off our only line of communication to Alpha."

"Which would still have been cut off if I hadn't fought off the vampires that attacked." Honestly, I didn't care; they'd either realize I hadn't done anything wrong or they wouldn't. Nothing I could say at this point was going to do anything to diminish the suspicion on me.

"True," she said. "I don't believe you're the one I'm looking for. But forgive me if I don't release you quite yet."

"I'll take it under consideration," I said, and turned to stretch my legs out on my cot, laying back down. "After all, I've got plenty of time to consider here. Not much else to do, but plenty of that."

She hesitated. "Would you like an e-reader? Something to help pass the time?"

"No," I said. "I don't really like to read anymore. I spent most of my childhood with nothing to do but read. And this is hardly the first time I've had to find something to do while locked in a metal enclosure for a few days."

She blanched at that one, and turned away. She took a couple robotic steps toward the door, then turned back. I heard it unlock for her, then swing open. "If you change your mind, just say so." She waited for me to respond, and when one wasn't forthcoming, she walked out, and the door shut behind her.

"I won't," I said to the empty room.

Chapter 18

The door opened again later that evening, and I thought maybe it was going to be dinner. I was wrong. I'd grown weary of the patterns of squares, of making different ones with my mind, of singing in my head (I was going to be damned if I gave them something to video behind the glass) and doing a few of the other things I did to pass time, and was ready for a visit again. Something, anything. When the door opened I hoped it would be Zack, oddly. Or Reed. It was neither.

"Come with me," Parks said, his gray hair hanging loose around his shoulders as always. He reminded me of Kris Kristofferson. Gruff, to the point, and then he stepped aside and left the door open.

I was sitting on my cot, and I stared at the open door for a minute after he vanished out of sight. I took a breath, sighed, then stood and followed. What else was I going to do?

When I reached the hall I saw he had already walked down it quite a ways. He didn't look back as he turned a corner, and I jogged to keep up with him. He moved pretty fast for an older guy, like the wolves he could so aptly channel gave him the ability to move faster as a man. I almost caught him by the time he reached the stairs, which were behind a heavy door. He didn't even hold it open for me, but I drew even with him by the time he reached the second landing. By the time we reached the fourth floor, I realized he was using his meta speed to outpace at a walk what most humans could do at a run. It would have been rude, I thought, if I had been a human trying to keep up with him.

We emerged not far from Ariadne and Old Man Winter's office. I could see through the windows that day was nearly done, that darkness had started to fall, giving me an idea of what time it was. There was still a light on in Ariadne's office and I entered in to find the members of M-Squad arrayed in an informal circle, with Ariadne at her desk. Eve was behind her at the window, staring out, Clary was bunched up in a seat that was way too small for him (every seat was way too small for him), Parks was standing at the door, gesturing for me to enter with an outstretched arm, and Bastian was leaned against the desk, his legs at a forty-five degree angle and his arms crossed. Reed was there, too, sitting in the other chair. He made to stand up, offering me his chair, but I waved him to sit down. "Why's everybody crammed in here? It's like a telephone-booth stuffing contest." When Ariadne gave me a blank look, I went on. "I dunno, they used to do it in the fifties or something, see how many people they can cram into a phone booth. If you'd like you could try it in my cell—"

"There she is," a voice came from the phone, and it caused me to freeze. "Mouthy as ever."

I looked down, and it took a moment before my mind made the full leap. "Mom?" I asked, truly uncertain.

"None other," she said, her voice echoing over the speaker. "I heard a rumor that they're keeping you imprisoned."

"Yeah," I said. "I'm starting to feel really at home here."

I could almost hear her teeth grind on the other end of the phone, but she didn't let me have it, surprisingly. Ariadne spoke up. "You wanted to speak with her, here she is."

"Plainly," my mother said. "So here's the thing. I have some blond dead weight that might be of interest to you – not much weight, I'll grant you, poor skinny thing – and not literally dead, either – yet – but if you want her back, I'll trade her for Sienna."

"Your daughter's not a hostage," Ariadne said, bristling.

"No, but she is a prisoner," my mother retorted, "which is why I'm proposing a prisoner exchange. Unless you'd like to argue that she's been free to come and go as she pleases while you've got her set up in the basement of your headquarters, feeding her one meal all day—"

Ariadne reached out and pressed a button to mute the microphone. "How does she know this?" Her face was contorted with rage.

"She was here," Bastian said. "She could have rigged our internal cameras. Or she could have a spy on the inside." He turned his gaze to Reed, who was still standing beside the empty chair, and who returned Bastian's look with a virulent glare.

"Hellloo?" my mother's voice came. "Is anyone still there? You could save the debate on how I know all this until after I get off the phone. That would be the courteous thing to do."

Ariadne stabbed down at the button, unmuting the phone. "Yes, we're here. Just so I understand, you suggest we trade Sienna for Kat?"

"You're not too bright, are you, Red?" my mother replied. "I bet Erich just loves dealing with that. Yes, that's what I'm suggesting. Do you think that you could handle so basic a transaction?"

Ariadne chewed on that for a moment. "Where do you want to meet? A public place—"

"Heavens, no," my mother said cheerfully. "I know where you are. Why don't we just meet on the lawn outside your headquarters building in three hours."

"Three hours?" Ariadne said. "Why—"

"Don't interrupt," my mother chided her. "Three hours. You can have your M-Squad there if you'd like, but all out where I can see them. If you try and capture me afterward, it'll end poorly for everyone involved."

"Are you threatening my people?" Ariadne asked, and I could see the irritation blanketing her.

"Yes. Keep up, will you? We're making a trade, on your turf, but my terms. So don't screw it up." There was a click on the other end of the phone and she was gone, followed by a dial tone.

"Get security on the perimeter," Ariadne said, and I could tell by the twist of her face she was steaming. "If she comes at us through any direction but the front gate, I want to know about it. Focus on the perimeter, double patrols, whatever you have to do; just don't…let her slip through."

"We should abandon the perimeter," Parks said and I watched as every head in the room swiveled to him. "It's a waste of resources. We need to protect the vital areas, like the dorms, headquarters and the labs. We only have so much force to go around and if we piss it away watching the fences, it weakens us. There aren't that many metas that could stop Sierra Nealon; she's too smart to come at this in a way we'd expect. She's got something else brewing and we won't be ready until it's too late if we spread out."

"Noted," Ariadne said, "and no. We will not abandon the perimeter and cloister in the buildings."

"Why?" Parks asked. "You want her to knock the hell out of our guards?"

"Because she's not the only threat we're dealing with!" Ariadne said. "In case you've forgotten, we're still at war with Omega."

"Whatever Omega throws at us is gonna cut through what we've got around the perimeter," Bastian opined. "The agents we have left wouldn't stop those vampires for longer than it'd take for them to feed."

Ariadne rubbed her temples as though in pain, her eyes closed. "There are too many elements at play here, and nothing makes sense. What is Sierra up to? What does she want?"

I blinked as the room fell into silence, and I thought about it. What did my mom want? Me, out of imprisonment? She'd never had a problem confining me to tighter spaces than I was in at the

Directorate's behest. She'd driven cross-country, from Wyoming, at least to get to an Omega facility in Wisconsin, just so she could...what? The only thing I'd seen her do was press a few buttons and—

"Andromeda," I said, and everyone looked at me. "That's all she's ever been interested in."

"She's about to give up her hostage to trade for you," Reed said, and his long hair was loose, partially eclipsing his face, but I could still see the slight incredulity. "I think she might be at least a little interested in what's happening to you."

"No, think about it," I said. "She drove cross-country to let Andromeda out. She didn't have a clue I'd be in Eagle River. And she seemed shocked that Andromeda was dead when I told her about that, like she couldn't believe it."

"Well, she's definitely dead," Ariadne said. "She hasn't so much as twitched since we brought her body back for study. And Doctor Sessions finished the autopsy yesterday, so if for some reason she was alive before without showing signs of it, she's certainly dead now that she's...uh..." She flushed, as though she were trying to steer around a delicate matter. "...been embalmed and...whatnot."

"You mean dissected." Reed didn't bother hiding his disgust, though it was a mild rebuke at best.

"I mean studied," Ariadne said, and flushed again. "The girl was dead. There's no reason not to learn as much from her as possible. She had powers that were abnormal even for a meta, not to mention being able to touch Sienna—"

I blinked. "Could that be it? Could that be why my mother was interested in her? Some way to tame the power of a succubus? Make us...touchable?"

"It makes more sense than anything else I've heard so far," Ariadne said, a pen up to her lips, chewing on the cap. "We'll need a guard on Sessions' lab, then."

"Then can we please pull off the perimeter and keep an eye on the places that matter?" Parks asked again.

"Yes," Ariadne said. "Fine. But I want constant communication between the guards. If someone goes silent I want everyone on them within a minute. None of this ridiculousness where we don't find out until later that we've lost a string of agents. Constant. Communication." She put emphasis between the words. "Got it?"

"Yes," Eve answered more abruptly than the others. "But you know, we don't have to let Sierra leave after the trade—"

"No," Ariadne said.

"Why not?" Eve's balding head flushed red at her cheeks, the new skin redder than her older, giving her head a blotchy look.

"Because," Ariadne said as she looked at me, "we're going to keep our word."

"Yes, ma'am," Parks said with a nod, and turned to file out of the office. Bastian followed him, and Eve began to extricate herself by walking around the length of Ariadne's desk. Clary stood and then turned toward me, looking down on me as though he had an eye on an insect. I watched him, and he jerked toward me as though he were about to hit me, but stopped after only the barest start to the motion. I kept my cool but glared at him, and he smiled in return, and let out a chuckle before walking past me and out the door.

"So am I going back to the confinement cell?" I asked, jarring Ariadne out of her thoughts. She put the pen down and I noted that the end of it had been worn to a nub by her teeth. "Or am I free to wander about the campus?"

"No to the first," she said, straightening up in her seat, "no to the second. I'll have you stay here in headquarters, but you can remain up here on the fourth floor while we wait. I'll have some food brought around since you haven't eaten." She picked up her phone and started to dial. "Want anything in particular?"

"Anything but meatloaf," I replied. She got a curious look on her face, then shook it off.

"How was your stay in the Chateau Directorate?" Reed asked me. He was still standing where he had during the meeting, only a foot away from me.

"The beds were poor, the food was terrible, and they didn't have turndown service," I said. "I think I'll book another getaway next weekend."

He smiled. "Good to see you're keeping a perspective on the whole thing. I'm not sure I'd be quite so forgiving if my employer had imprisoned me."

"What else was I going to do?" I asked. "Weep? Scream? Tear my hair out?"

"Leave?" he suggested. "Strike out on your own? Find something else to do with your life?"

I looked back at him, pondering a reply. "Jury's still out on all that. Looks like I'll be going with my mother for a while, anyway." I fumbled my hands, and reached into my pocket, where I felt the weight of the watch that had supposedly belonged to my father. I pulled it out and tried to slip it on my wrist, but it fell off and I caught it as it did so.

His face got inscrutable, and he looked down. "Nice watch," he said.

"This?" I raised it up. "Apparently it was my father's."

Ariadne hung up the phone. "Your father's? Where did you get it?"

"My mom left it for me," I said, "the other night when she snuck on campus."

"Are you freaking kidding me?" She was on her feet in an instant.

"No," I said. "It was on my bed when I got back—" My face went blank. "Oh. Wow, do I feel stupid."

"Give it here," she said, fingers out and beckoning. I gave it a last look of longing and let it fall into her hand.

"Be careful with it," I said, "in case it's real."

"I'm sure our tech guys will disassemble it with the utmost care," she said, "since it's probably laden with bugs. This is how she's finding out everything—"

"It's not," Reed said with a gentle shake of his head. He looked at the watch, still suspended from Ariadne's fingers, and drew my gaze there as well. "It's not from her mother. I left it there."

Chapter 19

"You?" I asked, and my mouth dropped open. "How…why?"

"You read my note?" He raised an eyebrow at me. "Your father would have wanted you to have it."

"You…you knew my father?" I stared at him hungrily. "You knew him?"

"I did," Reed said. "Before he died. He was the one who was responsible for me joining Alpha. He had been with them for years and years."

"I need a name," Ariadne said, sitting back down in her chair and sliding to the hutch behind her, where her computer waited.

Reed hesitated. "Jonathan. Jonathan James Traeger."

She blinked at him for a moment and then turned back to her computer, typing. "Jonathan James Traeger…hmmm…" She squinted and stared at the screen. "He was a handler for the Agency before it was destroyed." She looked up at me. "I would presume that's where he met your mother." She looked to Reed, who nodded. "Previous affiliations…hm…looks like he died in the attack that destroyed the Agency." She looked at Reed. "That doesn't really jibe with him working with Alpha."

"Actually, it does," Reed said. "He was working for Alpha the entire time, keeping an eye on the Agency. They were concerned the Agency was overstepping its bounds, suppressing metas' rights – which is something that tends to happen when a government becomes aware of metahuman existence and starts to view them as a threat."

"Were they?" I asked, genuinely curious. "Was the Agency killing them, on government orders?"

Reed shrugged. "Not really. I mean, they certainly made a few really bad ones disappear into a deep dark hole never to return – not unlike you guys – but I've read his...uh...Jon's reports, and they seem to point to an Agency with an almost pathological desire to avoid that sort of anti-meta trap that other governments have fallen into over the years. He thought it was because the Agency's upper management wanted to stay on the right side of it, that it wasn't an accident and that they tried to keep a good reputation among metas."

Ariadne looked at us, her smoky eyes making it hard to discern what she was thinking. "We've tried to do much the same. For metas that are awakened, that are aware of the world and whose parents have told them, there's a tight-knit underground community. Ruin your reputation and a lot of doors slam shut in your face; burning bridges like that can be a quick way to ensure you have to work five times as hard to get half as much done." She blinked. "At least that's the way the Director has always explained it."

"Whatever the reason," Reed went on, "Jon kept working with the Agency after his assignment for Alpha was completed." He turned to me. "It was because he met your mother."

I stared back at him, trying to process everything. A question popped to mind. "You said he's the reason you got into Alpha." Reed suddenly looked deeply uncomfortable. "How old are you?"

He seemed to let out a slight sigh of relief. "Twenty-five."

I frowned. "But then, when the Agency was destroyed, you would have been like seven—"

A beeping cut us off, the sound of Ariadne's cell phone going off. She blinked at it then picked it up and held it to her ear. "Yes?" Her eyes widened. "What?" She rolled in her chair backward to the window and looked out. "Son of a...all right." She pulled the phone from her ear and spun around to me. "Your mom is already here, waiting on the lawn with Kat."

"That was fast," Reed said. "She was on campus already when she called?"

"Or close nearby," Ariadne agreed. She looked to me. "You ready to go with her?"

My jaw tightened. "Not really. But I'm not all that excited to spend the rest of my life in a holding cell, either."

Ariadne looked down. "Fair point." She stood. "Let's get this over with."

"So that's it?" I asked as she made her way around the desk. She halted a couple feet from me and stared back as I spoke. "So long and best of luck?"

"This is not the end," Ariadne said. "But honestly, what do you want me to do? She's got one of our metas as a hostage, you're her daughter, and she's proposing a trade. Either you want to go with her or you don't. Either way, I need Kat back."

"And if I stay, what guarantee do I have that I don't get stuck back in the loneliest room in the house?" I set my jaw and readied for an argument of some sort.

"None," Ariadne answered. "Your fate with us hinges on whether we can find our traitor. Right now the evidence – however weak – points at you. Sorry." She shrugged. "You can either take your mother's opportunity and walk free, or stay and let us try to resolve this situation. Your choice."

"My choices suck," I said. "I've worked for you for six months and you haven't given me so much as the benefit of the doubt."

"Oh, but I have," she said. "More than once, in fact. I'm just keeping you out of a position to compromise our ongoing efforts. I don't think you're the traitor, but I'm double dumb if I'm wrong and I keep giving you the rope to hang us with." She folded her arms. "If you want to leave with your mom, do it. I wouldn't blame you. But don't ask me to stand back and not do everything I can, take every reasonable precaution I can to tamp down all the security threats we have hanging out there." Her mouth became a grim line. "So go, if you want. Stay, if you want. But know where you'll be if you do stay, because you'll be there until I can fix this situation."

I swallowed hard. "And what if you can't ever find the leak? The traitor?"

Her eyes hardened. "Then it's still in the hands of the Director what would be done with you. But don't imagine he's much more lenient than I am. Assume he'd be worse, as you make your decision."

I stared back at her, in the depths of her eyes, saw the feeling there beneath the gray, colorless exterior. "Are you telling me to go?"

She seemed to soften, her face falling. "Yes. Don't make me lock you up again. Just go. Get out of here. I'll find you once we find the traitor, and you can come back if you want. There's no point to you being confined here. Take your mother's out and get clear." She pressed the watch back into my hands, the edges pressing against my gloves.

I looked at her, then at the watch, and my face dissolved. "I don't have anywhere else to go."

With greatest reluctance, she took a step forward and I felt her arm around my shoulder, and she gave me a squeeze, careful not to touch me with her skin. "It doesn't matter. Just go. This is going very, very badly. We're losing this war with Omega, and it's not even close to the worst it can be. Your mother has been dodging Omega for years."

I pulled back from her, and felt the moisture in my eyes. "Okay."

She nodded at me, and I felt her hand on my back as I turned to look at Reed, who stared at me, impassive. "You know you always have another place to go."

"I might have to take you up on that," I said. "But...I guess we have something else to resolve first."

He raised an eyebrow at me. "You want me to come along?"

"Sure," I said, and led the way out the door, Reed and Ariadne a couple steps behind me. "Let's go see my mom."

Chapter 20

The elevator ride was quiet and long. The atmosphere hung heavy in the box, neither Reed nor Ariadne speaking as we went down. I, too, held my peace, with nothing left to say that hadn't already been said. When the tone dinged to let us know we'd reached the first floor, it startled me, sounding more than a little like a chime that precedes a bad announcement, like an impending execution.

I walked out the front doors of the headquarters building and saw a small assemblage waiting on the lawn. My mother was there, standing just behind Kat Forrest, who looked to be perfectly coiffed, her blond hair in order, her makeup applied like usual, her clothes in fine form.

I, on the other hand, was wearing the same clothes I had worn yesterday. My hair was mussed because I hadn't bothered fixing it since I slept on it earlier. I didn't wear makeup, so there was that.

My mother looked vaguely bored, studying her hands as though she were about to do her nails. Her dark hair was bound in a tight ponytail, just like she always wore it when we were sparring. She wore a black leather coat over a dark shirt, and tight jeans, much tighter than I would have felt confident wearing. Actually, they reminded me a little of Charlie. I realized with a shock, after a moment, that the reason she was looking at her fingernails was because she wasn't wearing any gloves, which was highly unusual in my experience. Breaking a house rule; not at all like Mom.

The four members of M-Squad were spread out in front of her, from Clary at the farthest left to Bastian next to him, then Kappler, and Parks at the far right. Every one of them was on edge, standing tense, except Clary, who was already shifted into a rocky skin, presumably to counteract my mother if she tried to touch him. Mom, for her part, seemed unconcerned by this show of force against her, and I wondered what sort of ace she had up her sleeve that allowed her to be so indifferent to the overwhelming numbers against her.

"Hi, sweetie," my mother said as we approached, looking up from her nails and giving me a fake smile, presumably more for the audience and less for me since I knew she was being false. "I was close by, so I figured why wait three hours when I could free my precious little baby now."

"You are such a bitch," I told her as I walked between Clary and Bastian to stand opposite Kat. I looked around my blond colleague to look my mother in the face as I said this.

"And you are awfully ungrateful seeing as how I'm getting you out of this little jam that your own bad decisions have landed you in." She said it mildly, without much concern either way. In the past, the level of smartassness I exhibited with the one sentence I had uttered to her would have landed me in the box for days without much in the way of leniency.

"Because you're playing at something else," I said, letting my recklessness run away with me again. "You don't care about getting me out except for as a means to an end. So what is it? You want Andromeda's autopsy report? Want to see the body yourself? What is it about her that's so important to you that you're willing to come out of hiding and move heaven and earth, break onto the Directorate campus over and over to find out?" I blinked at her. "What is it about her…" I choked and hated myself for feeling this much emotion and letting it come out in front of everyone. "…that's so important?" *That's more important than me?* – that was what I wanted to say.

I saw the slight wash of emotion over Mother's face, followed by the red flush of embarrassment. "This is not the time or place for…any of this." She cocked her head and looked past me. "What. The. Hell…are you doing here?"

I followed her gaze to where Reed stood not far behind my shoulder. "Confabbing," he said. "Trying to establish a tie between the Directorate and Alpha. What are you doing? Other than being a frightfully underwhelming parent to your daughter?"

I watched my mother's complexion turn even more scarlet as she reacted stronger than I would have imagined. "Oh, that's just…rich."

"I'm sorry…" I said, not actually apologetic so much as confused, "…but you two know each other?"

"Oh, I know him," my mother said, her face becoming a mask of barely controlled anger. I recognized it only because she was starting to get her emotions under control. She was usually cooler than that, but she had let slip, Reed's appearance causing her to let out something she hadn't intended to let out. "I doubt he'd remember me, since the last time I saw him was about twenty years ago."

"I remember you," Reed answered, stone-faced as well. "I'm kinda surprised you recognize me. It's been a while. I was just a kid, after all."

"You look just like him," my mother spat back at him. She seemed to calm. "Why do you remember me?"

I watched Reed as his eyes narrowed, and I saw a flicker of genuine pain cross his face. "I know I was young, but it's kinda hard to forget the day your dad introduces you to his new wife."

Chapter 21

"What…the…" I breathed. "You were married to…" I blinked. "Wait," I said to my mother, "you were married?"

"To your father," my mother returned. "Until he died."

"Then does that mean…" I blinked again, and turned to Reed, who gave me a shrug and a shake of the head. "You're my brother?"

Reed nodded. "Half, anyway."

Kat spoke up, drawing my attention along with everyone else's. "What…the hell is going on here? Can I go yet?"

"Stay where you are, Kitten," my mother snapped at her.

"My name is Kat!" A withering glare from my mother caused Kat to flinch. "Yes, ma'am," she said, chastened.

"So Sienna and this dude are brother and sister?" Clary piped up from behind me. "Cuz I thought I caught ro-mantic tension between them. Heh," he guffawed. "Guess it's more like BRO-mantic tension!" He burst out in uncontrolled laughter which was echoed by no one. "What?" He turned to Bastian. "Roberto, that is funny! Come on!"

I turned to Reed. "All this time you've been playing Leia to my Luke and you never told me?"

He frowned. "What? I'm totally Luke. You're the girl. Can you make objects move through the air?" He raised his finger and I felt a gust of wind blow my hair. "No? I'm Luke. You're Leia. Get it straight."

"So who's Han Solo?" Clary asked seriously. "And Darth Vader?"

"I'm going to kill every last one of you pathetic geeks," my mother said. "And I'm not even going to be nice about it. I'm going to just start draining souls. Will you please stop with the moronic Star Wars references? The movies came out in the 1970s. Most of you weren't even born then. Move on with your lives." She reached up and slapped Kat on the ass, causing the blond girl to jump. "Start walking. Sienna, get over here."

"You know," Clary said, "I think Kat should be Leia, because that gold bikini would look way better on her than Sienna."

I turned and gave him a glare. "I hate you, Clyde."

"Hey, girl! Ain't nobody calls me Clyde!"

"Sienna." My mother's tone snapped at me, drawing my attention back to her. Kat was already walking across the fifty or so feet of space between us. "Get over here."

I cast a look back at Reed and Ariadne, and caught muffled rage from Reed, directed at my mother. Ariadne was a bit more complex, stiff and impassive. I took a first hesitant step, then another, my feet carrying me toward Kat. The wind was warm, the dark skies and the light from the lamps nearby casting the only illumination on the whole scene. When I drew close to Kat, she stopped me, her hand on my sleeve. I looked down where it rested, then up to her wide, round eyes, sincere. "Don't go with her," she said quietly. "She's so...so...mean. So cold."

I looked at her, her perfect hair, her new clothes, her flawless makeup. "Why do you say that? Did she lock you in a metal box with no food and little water for days at a time?"

Kat's expression turned scandalized. "No!"

I felt a subtle shift in my emotions toward indifference, toward tiredness and uncaring. "Count yourself lucky. She must like you more than me."

"Sienna," my mother said warningly, a dark look on her face.

There was a beep behind me, urgent, and I stopped and turned to look. All motion seemed to freeze in the formation, and everyone turned to see what the noise was. It was Bastian's radio, and he held his hand up to his ear. "Yeah? Oh, damn." He looked up at Ariadne, sharply. "The vamps. They're here – we've got four men down by the dorms." A klaxon sounded in the distance and speakers all around the campus took up the warning, blaring as the spotlights activated on every building and we were flooded with light.

"Oh hell," Ariadne said, completely ruffled. "The entire population of metas – GO!" she shouted to M-Squad. "Don't wait, GO!" She fired a look at Kat. "They'll need you, too."

Kat looked back at me, and I felt a cool calm settle over me. She bit her lip for just a second before she took off after Clary and the others. Parks had already transformed, taking the lead as a wolf. Kappler was flying overhead, her usually invisible wings catching just enough light to reveal them against the dark, fluttering hard like a butterfly's.

"Reed…" Ariadne said, pleading, and I saw him look torn. The tension rose on his face, watching me, then he looked back to her. "We could really use your help." She looked at me. "We could use all the help we can get."

"I know what I'm in for if I stay," I told her. She nodded once, and started to run, wobbling in her heels, before she stopped and kicked them off.

Reed was the only one left now. Regret tinged his features. "Find me," he said, and I nodded. He thrust his hands down at the ground, and with a burst of air he shot up in a controlled leap that carried him a hundred feet along toward the dormitory building. Another blast of air cushioned his landing and then he launched off again.

"Well, wasn't that fortuitous?" My mother spoke from behind me, drawing my attention back to her. "I expected we'd have to fight our way out."

I looked at her warily. "What was your plan for that?"

She shrugged, as if she had not a care. "Fight our way out. Duh."

"Why are you here, Mother?" I asked, worn out and sick of all the emotion, revelation, wondering and worrying.

"I've got my reasons," she said, and I saw the skin crinkle at the edge of her eyes as she looked at me severely. "But you could do with a little more gratitude to me for saving your skin back at Eagle River, and again now."

"Thanks," I said without feeling. "But you're still not answering the question."

"I got what I came for. We can leave." She turned as if to emphasize that point, and started to walk away.

"What did you come here for?" I asked, taking a few steps to keep up. "Why are you here?" She was taking the path that wended toward the woods where I'd encountered her before. I waited for her to answer for a minute. "What is it about Andromeda that's so damned important?"

"You—" She whirled around and pointed a finger at my face. "You should learn to keep your mouth shut around others."

"So you were here for Andromeda," I said resignedly.

"Don't be ridiculous."

"What's ridiculous about reasoning?" I asked, and let my legs carry me past her along the path she had been walking. I heard her follow me, and I kept going. "You went halfway across the country to let her loose. You've exposed yourself to all sorts of danger coming here twice to..." I frowned. "Wait, you didn't know she was dead last time you were here." I turned to her. "What were you doing here then?"

She paused in her walk, stopping just in front of me. "Tapping Directorate communications so I could get Dr. Sessions' results from her physical exam, after he'd run it, and Zollers' psych exam results. I would also have loved to read the debriefing materials from after they questioned her – she'd have been a font of great information all around. Of course, I didn't know she was dead, so when I explored my tap later, I got autopsy results, which weren't what I'd hoped for." There wasn't an ounce of emotion from her.

"Why take Kat?" I looked at her, and she sighed, and started walking again. "Why take her with you? She seems like a liability, having to drag her along wherever you were going."

My mom waved a hand at me. "When you can render someone unconscious with a touch, having a hostage that fits neatly in your trunk is never a liability; it's an asset. Especially when your hostage is a meta, and your enemy is Erich Winter."

"You've got a grudge against Old Man Winter?" I was following her still, and she didn't say anything but I could see her demeanor change. "He acted like he didn't even know you when I asked him about you before; like you two worked at the Agency but didn't ever cross paths—"

She whirled around at me, eyes alight. "Did he now?" she asked, with a suppressed smile that was near maniacal in its intensity. My mother was not prone to displays of much emotion and I took a step back from her at the sight of it. "We knew each other. Of course we knew each other."

"Enemies?" I asked, and she shook her head. "Friends?" She shook it again. "Frienemies?" I tried again, and she looked at me like I was an idiot.

"We were acquaintances," she said. "But when the Agency was destroyed, we were two of the only survivors." She smiled. "Tell me something – when you're betrayed from the inside and your organization is destroyed, what do you think that makes the survivors?"

"I don't know," I said, not giving it a moment's thought. "Does it matter—"

"Suspects," she said, and I halted. "There were only three people that survived the destruction of the Agency. Me, Erich, and one other. And that makes every last one of us suspects. At least, in my mind." She shook her head. "I know I'm paranoid, and that you never accepted that I locked you in the house for any good reason, but I did. I swear I did. I had to keep you in the bounds, had to keep you hidden, because there's more going on here than you would believe."

"Why not tell me?" I asked. "Why not just be honest?"

"Oh, yes," she said sarcastically, "I should explain to my six-year-old girl that she can't leave the house because someday she's going to gain powers that will allow her to kill with a touch. I should tell her that any lifelong fantasies she might harbor about a normal life were a joke, a trick of a child's mind, and that – oh yes, this is the best – powerful forces from within that world of superhumans would want to capture her, to take her away from me, and turn her to their own purposes."

I let the silence hang between us. "Maybe if you'd given me a purpose of my own—"

She rolled her eyes and reminded me of Charlie again. "You didn't need a purpose at six, or sixteen. You needed to be kept safe from monsters like Wolfe and Omega...and worse. I would have told you when the time came."

"Why didn't you?" I asked. "Why did you just leave?" I looked at her, and I didn't even feel anything as I asked questions that had been on my mind for months. "You locked me in the box and you left, just left, didn't even say goodbye, or tell me what was happening, or—"

"I'm sorry," she said, and I saw genuine contrition. "I got waylayed by Wolfe, and I barely got away with my life. By the time I got free, I couldn't—" She stopped, broke off. "I did every-thing I could for you, I promise. And I'm still working for your benefit, even though you might not believe that—"

I would have responded but something stopped me, the same something that caused her to break off mid-sentence. Sound, movement, something fainter than the sirens going off in the dis-tance, warning us about danger that was supposed to be at the dormitory but instead was coming to us. The vampires, both of them, were moving toward us at speed.

"What the hell are those?" I heard my mother ask as she drew a gun from her waistband.

"Angel and Spike?" I suggested.

"Get behind me," my mother said as she stepped forward to block me from them.

"Unless you've got some sort of miracle bullets in there," I said, catching hold of her hand, "those will do nothing. They're vampires, and they don't take any sort of damage from guns."

She turned, whirling her head toward me, but I caught a hint of fear rather than anger. "Can we outrun them?"

I thought about it for a second. "No. But…" I turned and saw the training building not far from us, in the opposite direction of the vampires. "…we might be able to beat them if we had some weapons." I tugged on her arm and started to run. "This way!"

She looked for a second like she wanted to argue, but she didn't, taking up with me as we ran for the training facility. I didn't slow as we approached, and saw the vamps gaining on us. We came up on the door of the building, the glass front, and I wondered if it was unlocked.

My mother raised her gun and fired, bullets shattering the glass panes of the door. I flinched and hesitated, fearful that the bullets were going to ricochet back at me. After five shots the glass fell out, breaking into pieces that covered the ground. I flew through the hole in the middle of the door, slowing down to make sure I didn't trip. Mother followed, the vamps only about a hundred feet behind us. "Over here!" I called to Mom, and dodged toward the practice room, opening the glass door and running inside, cutting across the open mats and stopping at the wall of weapons. I stared up and cast a look back at Mom, who was waiting at the door.

"Sword," she said, nodding at the broadsword on the wall next to me. I tossed it to her and grabbed the katana for myself. I ran to join her by the door as we heard movement in the hallway. "You take the ugly one," she whispered.

I was about to question her on which one was the ugly one when I noticed the smile creasing her lips. "Did you just make a joke?"

"It seemed the appropriate time."

The glass window to the hallway exploded behind me and I turned to see Blondie enter through it, glass filling the air around me as a rain of broken shards was came down sideways. I held up an arm to protect my face and spun backward to avoid the worst of it. In that moment, I heard the door slam open and my mother spring to action against the second vamp. I heard a great exhalation of breath from her as she swung her sword and I heard it hit flesh. After that I was done listening because the first vampire was in front of me and I had a fight of my own to deal with.

I raised my blade as he feinted toward me, catching him on the wrist and opening it. Whether he noticed or not was open to debate, because he didn't react at all, pushing hard against the edge of the blade and sending it back at me, knocking me off balance as he did so. I came up and got a good look at his jagged teeth, formed into a smile under blond hair that looked bleached, and a face that was so lacking in humanity it made Wolfe look like a compassionate school guidance counselor by comparison. He pursued me and I tried to step back, but off-balance as I was, it turned into a hop as I tried to buy time.

It worked enough to let me get my footing, but he was still coming, so I poked at him, at the chest, and the tip of my sword bit into his dark shirt and the flesh beneath. I turned it into a hard, ramming motion that again elicited no reaction, but I pushed and he stumbled back from the force, as though I had shoved him with my hand instead of a pointed blade. Still, he made no noise; the only sound in the room was my breathing and my mother's, somewhere behind me.

I took the attack to him, swinging my sword as he used his hands to block, that soulless grin still exposing his teeth. Every strike opened his flesh, but no blood dripped out, and I watched as the skin seemed to pucker and bind back together before my eyes. I made a dance out of my sword, practicing a kata of my own creation, a free-flow of motion, the sword spinning in my hands. I went low, hacking at the legs, wondering if I cut the muscles if it'd slow his motion. I buried a strike in his knee and he wobbled before recovering and slicing me across the shoulder with a slash of claws that caused the fabric of my shirt to rip at the sleeve.

I whirled in a circle and came at him low again, catching him in a perfect strike across the back of the knee that cut his leg out from under him – not literally, but the force of my blow was so great that when the blade had bitten in, it reached the bone. When the momentum of my attack had nowhere else to go it pulled his leg from the ground as though I had performed a leg sweep.

The vampire stumbled, now on one leg. Sensing his predicament, I launched into a side kick that would have killed a human, hitting him in the head with it. As it was, the vampire lost his footing and hit the far wall, shattering one of the mirrors and landing on his face.

I leapt to exploit the advantage and landed on his back, driving my sword into it. I felt the impact up my arms as I drove home my blow, the tip of the blade striking and sticking against his ribs, its momentum halted. The shock of the attack caused him to whiplash and it drove his head into the mat, from which it rebounded up, a jarring motion of the spine that would have killed a normal person by breaking their neck.

His neck.

I heard the voices whisper in my head, Gavrikov and Wolfe, giving me the answer I sought. It took me only a moment to grasp their meaning and I dropped to my knees, straddling the vamp's back as I grabbed the dulled edge of my blade and slid the sharp edge against his throat and pulled.

The blade cut through the tissue without effort, then stopped, halted by a spine that was strong, as though it was steel. His hands came up and seized mine, trying to stop them, but he had no leverage. I pulled, and felt the blade stir another centimeter, then another, ignoring the lancing pain in my hands as he clawed at them, tearing through my gloves and into my skin, ripping at my sleeves and my wrists.

I felt the last tug cut through and the hands tearing at me went limp as the sword burst free from the back of the vampire's neck. I fell onto the mat as something heavy that wore a patch of blond hair bounced off my chest. I batted it away with a free hand. Yuck. I scrambled to my feet to see Mom and the raven-haired vampire locked in battle. She was giving him about eight different kinds of hell and he was giving it right back. I angled myself to come up from behind him as she was falling back from a wave of his attacks. I struck as he was moving forward, a hard swing to the back of his neck that sent him to the floor face-first. I followed up with a repeat of what I'd done to the other vampire.

Mother stood back and watched as I pulled, again, hands forcing the blade against his throat until I finished and fell backward again, similar to the last time, this time not bothering to get up immediately. I lay on my back, breathing hard from the exertion of what I'd just done. I saw a hand reach down. I looked up and took it, and Mother helped me to my feet. "Nice work," she said, looking at the two separate bodies that lay on the mats. "I ran across a vampire a long time ago, when I was working with the Agency." She frowned. "Had to use a flamethrower to put that one down."

"Yeah, I used a flaming club to take it to these two the last time I fought them," I said, peeling the shredded gloves off my hands to examine the damage they'd done to my skin. The gouging wounds left by their claws were mostly superficial, but they still stung. "Tough bastards, though."

"Yeah," she said, and nodded. "We should get going."

I sighed. "I don't want to go with you."

I saw a veil slide down behind her eyes, whatever momentary pride she was feeling evaporated. "We're leaving. Together. You are coming with me."

I felt something like steel run down the length of my spine and I pushed my chest out as I stood up straight. The air was heavy in the room, like summer humidity was creeping in from the window we'd broken out front. "No, I'm not."

"You will," she said again, her voice rising, "and—" Her hand came up and then she jerked, twitching hard and falling to her knees. As she dropped, I saw two little threads trailing off her back and leading to someone standing behind her, in the shadows, a taser extended from a shadowy hand.

He stepped into the light the moon cast across the floor from the windows, and I recognized his face. "Sorry to interrupt this moment of mother-daughter bonding," Michael Mormont said with a malicious grin, "but I'm afraid I'm going to have to insist that the two of you aren't going to be going your own way." His mouth twisted, and his eyes slipped into the shadow as his grin became more perverse. "You'll both be coming with me."

Chapter 22

I did get up off the basement floor, eventually. I went upstairs and showered, a long one that lasted over an hour. I scrubbed myself clean of the accumulation of waste and stink that I had gathered in the time I'd spent in the box. After that, I sat down in the tub and let the hot water run over me, let it tap at my skin, on my head, felt the warmth as it washed over me.

I took deep breaths in through my nose and out through my mouth; I read that helped purge strong emotion. The smell of the chlorine in the tap water was faint, but I welcomed it. The aroma of the box lingered, even after the repeated scrubbings, and all I wanted was for it to go away.

I ate after that, sitting at the table in the kitchen alone, the quiet almost overwhelming. I kept the lights off. The only source of illumination was the sun slipping through the cracks from behind the blockaded windows. I ate the turkey sandwich I made for myself one slow bite at a time, tasting the bread, the mayo and the meat, and trying to keep myself from wolfing it down after going without food for almost a day. The dull colors of the walls of the house weren't visible in the dark, but the lack of light was oddly soothing.

Once I had eaten, I found myself in mother's bathroom, staring at the checkered tiles – one little black one every four white ones, in square patterns. The room was small, closet-sized, with an old countertop, and porcelain toilet. There was only one shower in the house, and it was in the bathroom Mother referred to as mine.

She did everything else in her own bathroom, though, and there was long, brown hair gathered around the white baseboards in knots, as though it had fallen and somehow gathered itself together and tied itself up.

I took the heavy cleaners from the kitchen and scrubbed the sink, the toilet, the vanity and the floors. The sharp smell of the chemicals was heavy in my nose, and I felt lightheaded. The toilet had a permanent ring on the inside of it where the water line rested, and no matter how hard I scrubbed, I could never seem to get that faded yellowish ring off. Today I tried harder than most.

I took a brush out next, a small one for scrubbing floors, and I started rubbing at the tile. It should have been easy, should have been simple. I scrubbed as I thought about what I'd done, what I'd said, what she'd said back. I took another breath, heavy, in through the nose, out through the mouth, and kept scrubbing.

I thought about the box, all the times I'd been locked in it, and I rubbed at the tile. There was a dark spot on the floor between the wall and the toilet. I wrestled myself in the gap between them, almost wedging myself in, and started to scrub, going so far as to clean the corrosion and lime off the valves that shut off water to the toilet. I focused again on the spot on the floor, which was under where the plunger rested. I scrubbed harder, seeing the ring fade slightly with the effort.

I pushed harder, the last little bit of it resisting, standing out from the white tile. I heard something crack, and felt a sharp sting, pulling my hand back as though I'd touched a lit eye on the stove. I looked at my palm and watched a trickle of blood run down it. My hand; the recurve handle of the scrubbing brush had broken off, and the plastic edge that remained was sharp enough that it had stabbed me when it broke.

I hurried my hand under the sink and turned on the water. I watched the clear liquid turn red as it ran over my wound and down into the white porcelain basin, rinsing the blood down the drain. I watched it swirl, catching the light, and after a few minutes I pulled my cold hand out. The blood had started to clot, and I put a bandage over it, taking care to treat it gingerly, taping it carefully to my skin. Once I was done, I held it up in the mirror in front of me.

I saw my face for the first time since I'd gotten out of the box that morning. Dark circles rested under my eyes, and they were swollen and puffy. My hair was frizzed, because I'd not bothered to straighten it with the flatiron after getting out of the shower. I usually did, because Mother got upset when I let myself slip in hygiene; it wasn't disciplined to let oneself go, she'd say.

I heard movement out in the living room, the familiar beep of the alarm system turning off, and I jerked in automatic motion. I hurried to pick up the bucket and cleaning supplies, throwing the broken scrub brush into the garbage can and jamming my hands back into the gloves I'd taken off to clean; breaking a major rule, even for ease of cleaning, was a big no-no. I took a quick look, inspecting my handiwork, and realized I had been cleaning for three hours.

I came down the hall to find Mother standing in the dining room, looking at several envelopes in her hands. She was frowning at them, concentrating, and one after another she threw them in the trash can. I brushed past her without saying anything, and stowed the cleaning supplies back under the sink. She tossed another envelope into the garbage and I started past her again when she spoke. "We're going to do martial arts practice in five minutes." She let a postcard drop into the garbage and raised her head to look at me. "Did you hear me?" I nodded, and she shook her head as I headed toward my room to change into workout clothes.

The workout was long and focused on katas. I did the same one, over and over, working on my breathing as she watched me, calling out criticism where she felt it was warranted. I executed every move as crisply as I could; blows strong enough to hurt and kill were the standard. Weak hits, anything that looked pretty but lacked force, were called out, and my punishment was to do push-ups. I stared at the blue mats as my arms pumped up and down and my breath cycled in through the nose, out through the mouth. I let out a last breath as I finished my ten push-up punishment, and snapped back to my feet. Laggardly behavior carried its own sort of punishment – more push-ups.

"All right," Mother said, her arms folded, her navy nylon gym pants clashing against her white t-shirt. Her complexion was darker than mine, partly due to her exposure to the sun and partly due to genetics. "I can see we've got some work to do on strength training, but we'll save that for another time." Her eyes narrowed as she surveyed me. I stood at a ready position, my hands in front of me and my body stiff at attention. "We need to work on precision; you're getting sloppy."

My eyes followed her as she started to move, but I felt a burning inside. Deep breath in through nose, out through the mouth. She walked to the wall and pulled a katana from the pegs and tossed it to me. I reached out and caught it, whipping it around in a wide arc and then returning to a ready position again. I avoided cringing on the upswing; the hilt was mashing against my bandage, and I felt the wetness of blood as my cut tore open under my gloves.

"You'll do your entire form with the sword," she said, arms folded again now, taking one small step at a time, as though she were about to circle me. "Crisp, perfect, and with every attack I had better see the appropriate amount of force." She waved a hand in the air. "This is an exercise in control. It's not a butcher's knife, and it needs to be guided properly."

I nodded and began my kata. Each move, I tried to focus, tried to keep my eyes on the place where my sword was going. I tuned out the pain, the dull, stabbing feeling that came as I wrapped my hand tight around the hilt. Mother didn't help; she was hovering, following me around. Three times I turned to deliver my next at-tack and was forced to deviate as she placed herself in my path.

"Testing your control," she said, stepping out of the way each time – after I had altered my kata to avoid her. Each move caused me pain, as I held the sword in the hand that wore the bandage. I felt blood dripping down my wrist and into my sleeve. Mother had little tolerance for anything but perfection, and admitting that I had hurt myself might reveal that I had been cleaning with my gloves off – which meant the box, again. I was holding my breath now, as much as possible, trying to bottle up the pain. Beads of sweat rolled down my face in a trickle, and I swore they might have been blood as well, as though the pain were everywhere and the blood was too.

I came to a finish and I heard slow clapping start behind me. I turned my head, still frozen in my last move, sword extended, one of my legs far in front of the other. The clapping was maddeningly slow, like a mocking laugh. She put her hands together over and over, letting seconds hang in the air between each clap.

I felt my face redden, as though the blood that wasn't running down my arm was rushing to it, felt the heat in the room turned up to twelve. My breathing exercise wasn't working to purge the emotion anymore; the feeling was too strong. I held myself in place, but I felt my hand shake with the sword in it. I knew my face was betraying me, but I couldn't hold back the tide of emo-tions. I let my feet drift back to a closed stance, shoulder-distance apart, and I brought the sword up.

My mother raised an eyebrow, a subtle motion, but she stopped clapping, and she fixated on my sword. "What are you planning to do with that? You know what it means if you point it. It's not a butcher's knife, but still you wave it around like—"

I flung the sword, felt the hilt release from my hand with one last sharp stab to my palm, and I heard it hit the wall with a clatter and bounce off as I ran at her. My fists were balled up, my rage coming from deep within, somewhere that a million breaths out through the mouth could never expel. I hissed as I came at her, dropping into a low stance as I readied my first attack. I was not thinking, I had no plan, no intention but to hurt her, to hit her and drive the arrogance out of her, to make her feel the same pain she kept pushing on me. I watched her register surprise just before I landed my first blow, and I knew it would be sweet.

It lost its sweetness as she sidestepped out of the path of my strike, moving so quickly I didn't even see her do it. She landed a punch to my jaw that caused my head to snap back, and I saw a flash of blackness before I came back to myself. My legs felt like rubber bands that I was trying to stand on, unable to support my weight. She hit me again, this time in the belly, in the solar plexus, and I lost all the wind out of my lungs, expelled in one loud noise – through the mouth. I cradled my stomach as I hit the mat without concern for the cushion I was landing on.

I stared up at the ceiling, still holding my midsection, trying to regain my breath but failing, wheezing. I knew cerebrally that I wasn't dying of asphyxiation, but it felt like I was, like I couldn't get enough air to my brain or my body, that I was going to die gasping right there on the mat.

Mother stood above me, arms crossed, calm and collected, unmoving. "You've got spirit," she said, looking at the black gloves she wore, the same kind she always forced me to wear, "but spirit won't get you anything save for a nasty death." She squatted next to me, and I felt her glove on my arm. "Discipline. Control." I looked into her eyes as she stripped my glove off, baring my bandaged palm. "Obedience." She shifted position and gripped me under the armpits, lifting me up. I saw the box in the corner, she faced me toward it, its wide maw open as if ready to swallow me up, and I tensed in her arms.

She gripped my wrists, lifted my hands above my head and I felt the pain begin to subside, deep breaths flooding into my lungs.

It still hurt, I still had trouble breathing, but it got better. "Breathe," she said, as I stared at the box, taking deep breaths, all through my mouth, every one of them. "Get your breathing under control. You don't want to hyperventilate."

Her grip on my wrists faded and my legs took up their own weight again. I stared into the box, into the shadows and darkness inside, and realized I couldn't see the back of it, not even with the lights on. It waited for me, a silent mouth ready to devour me whole. I turned my head, slow, fearful. Mother was still standing directly behind me, close enough that I could smell her sour breath, like rancid milk.

"Spirit won't get you anything but killed," she said to me again, and her face was blank, an empty reservoir of no emotion. "You use your strength by putting your emotions on a leash." She looked down, then back up at me again, and I could have sworn she shifted her feet, as though from nervousness. "You will obey. You will listen. There are rules for a reason."

"I just..." I choked out. "I just...I needed to...I felt..."

"I don't care," she said with a slight shake of her head, and by the total neutrality of her voice I could tell she meant it. "Feelings are irrelevant. Feelings won't change anything; action will." She took a step back from me, and turned toward the stairs. "Follow the rules, not your feelings." She cast a look back as she reached the bottom of the stairs. "Your feelings will lead you to make stupid decisions – like they just did. Listen. To me, to the rules. Ignore your instincts; they'll get you killed." She cocked her head at me. "Like they almost just did."

I watched her head bob back, as though she were looking down her nose at me, surveying me coldly, and then she disappeared up the stairs, head first, then torso, until her feet receded from view and I was left by myself in the basement.

Chapter 23

Now

"You jackass," I said, and Mormont raised his other hand to reveal a gun. "You didn't have to do that."

"I think I did," he said, and I watched Mom writhe again as he pushed a button on the grip of the taser. "This is a taser built specifically for metas, so it holds a lot higher charge than the civilian models sold for use on humans." He seemed to be talking to my mom. "It has a over a dozen charges, so I can keep you writhing in pain until you pass out, or you can just accept that I can drop an elephant with it and we can go on about our business without me having to push the button again."

"Oh…okay," my mother said, from her hands and knees. "But gosh…I sure was enjoying…those lovely…zaps of electricity."

"And she wonders why I smart off at her?" I asked.

Mormont's grin faded and I saw him thumb the trigger again as my mother jolted and fell to her face. "No one likes a smartass," he said when she finished writhing. "You done?"

"I'm ready to start if she's finished," I said.

He waved the gun at me. "I hear so much as a word out of your mouth, I'm just going to fill you full of bullets and drag you to the car. I'll let them sort you out later."

I stiffened at his words. "Your car? You're not planning on taking us to the confinement cells?" I watched him, and something connected before he even reacted. "You're the spy! Oh, you bastard!" His eyes narrowed and his gun stopped waving at my insult, pointed instead at my heart. "Did I say bastard?" I felt the heat of emotion run through my veins. "Yeah, well, I meant it. You ran that interrogation on me and messed with my head when all along it was you?"

He rolled his eyes. "You sound surprised."

I opened my mouth to answer, then after a moment's thought: "I probably shouldn't be. So, you work for Omega?" I felt my nostrils flare in irritation. "You turned the vamps loose too, then?"

"Yes," he said with a narrow smile. "My boss won't be too happy that they died before I could stop you, but I'll smooth that out a little by delivering a second succubus." He stroked the trigger again and Mom rolled in another jolt of electricity. I started to make a move toward him and he cocked the hammer of his pistol. "Watch it. You can take a lot of bullets before you die, and every one of them will hurt, I promise." He gestured with the gun. "Drop the sword."

I felt my fingers clench on it, not wanting to surrender my only weapon. "Why? You afraid you can't shoot it out of my hands before I jump at you and slice your face off?"

"Don't insult us both by patronizing me," he said, and I heard the threat in his words. "Drop it now, or I'll put you on the ground and drag you out of here in a bloody heap."

I smiled thinly as I held out the sword and dropped it to the mat. "But you'd rather do things the easy way."

"Always," Mormont said, and reached down with the hand that held the taser to fetch something off his belt: heavy duty handcuffs I recognized from when he had placed them on me came up in his hand, two pairs, and he tossed them at me. I caught them easily and held them up. "Put them on your mother, then put the other pair on yourself. Slowly. Any sudden moves and you'll be picking lead out of holes in your body for the next two weeks."

I sauntered forward, trying to convey defiance with my posture as I came up to my mom but kept my glare firmly rooted on Mormont. "I hope you're at least getting a big fat cash bonus for this."

Mormont smiled tightly. "You have no idea."

"Oh?" I leaned down to where my mother lay, her face pressed against the mat. "I'm worth a lot to Omega?"

"An inconceivable amount," he replied. "About ten million."

I paused and looked up at him, letting out a low whistle. "Dollars?" When he nodded, I arched my eyebrows in surprise. "Wow. Wonder how much they'll pay you for two succubi?"

"I don't know," he said. "This one has some miles on her."

"And yet still," my mother said from all fours, "I'll find it in me to run you over, you pr—" There was a hissing noise as Mormont pulled the taser's trigger again and Mom collapsed onto her face, writhing.

"Even if it's not double," Mormont said, as casual as if he hadn't just run voltage through a living, breathing human being, "it'll be enough to live comfortably for a nice long time, far from whatever petty disputes you've got going on here."

"You can't run far enough or fast enough to get away from this," came a voice from the broken door. I saw a hand reach in as a figure followed. I tried to breathe a sigh of relief but I caught myself. Dr. Quinton Zollers stepped onto the broken glass, feet crunching with every step, a pistol aimed at Michael Mormont. "Unless you think you can outrun a bullet?"

"Doc," Mormont said with a grim look that never left him, even as the gun still pointed at me, "don't make me kill this girl. If she comes with me, she'll at least be alive – that's how Omega wants her." He thumbed the hammer again, for emphasis, and I heard it click as he decocked and recocked it. "But if you push me, I'll put her brains all over that wall before you can—"

"Then you'll have Omega after you and pissed off as well as the Directorate." Zollers didn't flinch. "I'm a counselor, and as such I'd advise you not to get yourself killed here, because if you harm that girl, you're a dead man, even if I don't kill you, and you know it." Zollers raised his pistol, looking down the sights at Mormont. "So...do you want to die today? Because if you shoot her, you're signing your own death warrant. Put the gun down."

Mormont pursed his lips. "I'm not gonna just disappear into the Arizona desert."

Zollers didn't blink. "You're either going to the prison under the ground or you're going under the ground. Your choice. Make it quick. My finger is starting to itch."

Mormont was still, for just a moment. "In that case—"

I didn't hear his last words, blotted out as they were by gun-shots, as Zollers emptied his gun into Mormont, every shot echo-ing through the room as loudly as if it were fired with the barrel right by my ear. I dodged out of the way, pulling my mother back to the ground with me. Mormont's gun fired twice as his muscles contracted one last time.

There was a heavy smell of gunpowder in the air as the smoke began to swirl. I lay on the ground next to Mother, and I watched Mormont collapse onto his back, unmoving. I rolled to him and yanked the gun and taser out of his grasp. There was no sign of movement on his face and he had already stopped breathing. There were a series of red circles spreading out of holes in his torso. I was reminded of Andromeda again as I watched one of the wounds bleed, blinking as his white shirt turned red beneath his suit coat.

I looked up at Zollers, his calm eyes looking at the dead man next to me, his pistol still pointed at Mormont, and by extension of my proximity to the body, me. "Doc?" I asked, jarring him back to himself. He stared down the sights at me, and I caught a flicker of something in his eyes that scared me. "Doc? You can put the gun down now."

He stared hard down the sights at me for another long few seconds before his arm started working again and the pistol ratch-eted down, slowly, a little at a time until it was by his side. He then seemed to take a breath, finally. "Never did trust that son of a bitch," he said with a nod at Mormont.

"Have you ever killed anyone before?" I asked, getting to my feet.

"No," he said, staring at the body. "No, I haven't. Counseled a lot of people about it, though." He laughed, a little rueful. "You'd think that would have prepared me for how it'd feel, hearing them talk about it, but…" He wore a smile that wavered, then disappeared. "…it really doesn't."

I felt a little pity for him, though I didn't know where from. I had killed before, and I hated it. I cast a look at the two dead vampires on the mats, and realized I didn't really feel that bad for them because they were beyond subhuman, but I had regretted it when I had to kill Gavrikov. I even felt bad about killing Wolfe, though I could barely admit it to myself, let alone fathom where the hell that infinitesimally small remorse came from. "It's okay," I said to him for the first time, and meant it, almost as repayment for all the times he'd told me the same. "You might want to put the gun down," I told him as I watched his hand shake. He looked down at it and his fingers unclenched. The pistol fell from his grasp and to the mat as he stared at it. I watched him, saw his eyes widen and his head jerk up a moment before a taser swung around and hit him in the side of the head as he tried to dodge.

I whirled and saw Mother holding the taser by the prongs that had been lodged in her skin. She dropped it to the ground. "I didn't really want to knock him out like that," she said, and I looked – Zollers was facedown on the mat, eyes closed – "but I need Directorate complications right now like I need another hundred thousand volts." She centered her gaze on me. "Let's go."

"I'm not going with you," I said, already down and checking on Dr. Zollers. I touched him briefly with my ungloved hands, long enough to establish he had a strong pulse and was still breathing, but no more than a couple seconds. "Are you insane? He just saved us from being kidnapped by Omega."

"And that's all well and good," she said, and I felt her come up to my shoulder, "except that the next logical step would be for us to be confined in our own private cells by the Directorate instead." I looked up and saw her blue eyes flash cold. "And I personally am not looking to be a prisoner of Erich Winter. Not now, not ever." She reached down and I felt the pressure of her hand on me, on the shoulder, squeezing my arm, tugging me to my feet. I came up and threw it off.

I watched her eyes blaze in reaction when I did it, and I planted my feet as she stared at me. "I'm not going with you."

"I guess you've forgotten what happens—"

"When I break the rules?" I asked. "When I don't follow your commands?" I circled her and she circled me, keeping our distance in a staredown unlike anything I'd done with her before.

"Everything I do, I do for your own good," she said, and it poured a little more gasoline on the fire inside me. "The things I do for you, even now, with Andromeda, are for your future—"

"You still treat me like a child," I said and stopped circling, causing her to do the same. "Feed me a line about rules, or how it's all for my own good, and stop short of trusting me with the truth." I smiled, and tried to make it devastating. "All these years and you're still trying to keep me in a little box in the dark."

She took a step forward and caught me flatfooted. It was stupid for me to be so smug that I didn't expect her to come at me, but I didn't, and she landed a slap on my cheek that sent me into a turn and a fall that I rolled out of when I hit the mat. I came to one knee near the wall and looked down at something next to me, and realized it was the katana. I looked at her, then at the sword, and picked it up and pointed the blade toward her, staring down the sleek metal surface, at my reflection in it, distorted and rounded. Then I looked up at her, at the shock on her face.

"So that's how it is?" She stared at me in disbelief, then I watched the emotion dissolve into a cold fury. "All right." She looked around and found the broadsword a few feet to her left and stooped down to pick it up, pointing the blade at me. "You know what this means, right?"

"You don't point a blade at anything you don't mean to have dead," I said grimly.

She stared at me and I could feel the electricity between us as though the taser were firing from her eyes to mine. "So you haven't forgotten."

I stared down the blade at her. "I haven't forgotten."

She watched me as I rose to my feet, the sword never wavering. "Then it's on you, what happens now," she said. Before I could respond, she was in motion, her blade leaping at me. I parried, spinning to the side, surprising her and batting her weapon away. She came at me again and I dodged, riposting from the side and catching her with a glancing blow that elicited a grunt of surprise and pain. I took a step back, my blade still aimed at her, and I let a smile cross my lips. "Been practicing?" she asked.

"You don't think I've just been sitting around watching TV and dating boys the last six months, do you?" I asked. I whipped the sword around to a defensive posture above my head in a flashy move that was crisp and beautiful and could have been pulled out of the katas she used to teach me.

A smile crossed her lips. "I suppose I sort of did."

I darted forward with the sword, clashing with hers as she retreated from my onslaught. I hit my blade against hers, chipping metal from both, and hammered it again, causing her to flinch from the strength of my attack. "Then I guess that makes you kind of an idiot, doesn't it?" I plunged the sword for the third attack, this time connecting hard with her hand, and she let out a cry of pain as her weapon flew out of reach and she bent at the waist, holding her injured hand.

I was prepared to halt my attack when she sprang at me over

the distance of two feet, all that remained between us, and batted my sword aside, putting her hands against my face, pressing her bloody hands onto my cheeks as we both toppled over. I hit the mats and bounced, throwing my hands up in defense and against her face as I braced for it; the pain that I had inflicted upon others, the pain of the stronger succubus, my mother, beginning to take my soul. I fought against her, pushed at her, but she doggedly clung on and I moaned and squealed as I fought to get free.

I felt the press of her flesh on mine, of her touch against my cheek as she straddled me and pushed down. I reached up and wrapped my hands around hers, tugging on her wrists, trying to pull them free, but they didn't budge. I waited for the pain to swarm me, overwhelm me the way I'd seen it take Wolfe, the way it had pulled at Gavrikov, ripping their souls free of their bodies, starting with a little jolt and building to a crescendo of agony that tore their very essence from their bodies and lodged it in my brain. I felt a slight stir in my skin as she clung tight, and I waited, still fighting, an agony building in my lungs more from the anticipation in my mind than the real pain in my body.

I watched her face, like it was a snapshot being shown to me, a moment frozen in time, and the cold fury broke over it as she grimaced, at first, then cried out in pain and tried to jerk her hands away. Mine were on hers, though, and I gripped her tight, felt the swirl begin in my mind as I overpowered her. I rose almost without realizing it as she fell back, trying to pull her hands away from mine. I held on, even as she started to scream, until finally she jerked once more and tugged free, staggering back onto the mats and landing on her backside as I stared down at her and she looked up at me. Her face was haggard, blue eyes fearful for the first time since I'd known her.

"So," she said, recovering her frosty expression, "it's you. You're the more powerful."

"You're damned right I am." I looked down at her, my expression now a cold fury not unlike hers. "Look at you. My whole life you tried to keep me under your control. You had to beat me down, cage me – to keep me from rising." I looked at her with the ultimate disdain. "No more. I'm not a little girl anymore. And you...will...never...have power over me again. You will never tell me what to do again."

I heard movement from the door and it creaked open as Scott and Kat slid in. Kat dropped to her knees by Zollers, her expression all concern. Reed was three steps behind them, and halted next to Scott as they stared at the sight of me standing over my mother, still on her knees. "Sienna," Scott said, looking at the carnage, the three dead bodies and the fallen psychiatrist, "you okay?"

"Never better," I said, still staring down my mother.

"You'll regret this," Mother said, looking up at me with flames in her eyes. "You'll be sorry you stayed. There's a storm coming, and it's gonna sweep away the old order of metas. You, this place, you're going to be sitting in a ruin, and when you look back on this moment, I want you to remember." She stood as she said it, and looked me dead in the eye. "I did it all for your own good, and I tried to show you the way, but you didn't listen."

I stared back at her. "I've listened to you long enough. I'll find my own way, through whatever storm comes."

She shook her head, and in her eyes there was a cold satisfaction that bordered fear. "No you won't. Not this one. I don't care how strong you are; you're not ready for this. You won't be able to handle it alone."

"She's not alone," Scott said from behind her, eliciting a glare from my mother. "She's got us."

"And who are you?" my mother asked with a scoffing amusement. "The M-Squad Junior League?"

"No," Scott said. "Unlike you, we're family."

"Family," my mother said with a derisive laugh. "You're not

family. That's a word used by simpering losers to make themselves feel better about their pitiful relationships. You're not family; you're a bunch of puppets that Erich Winter has dancing in a
pretty little row to whatever tune he's playing."

"Maybe," I said, "but Erich Winter has trusted me with more
truth in six months than you have in eighteen years." I took a step
closer to her. "And when push comes to shove – and if what you
say is true, it will – I'd rather have these three at my side than
you." I stuck out my chin at her. "I'd rather be Sienna, the Directorate agent in charge of her own destiny, than the girl in the box,
waiting for her mother to turn her loose someday."

Mom took a step back, as though I'd hit her. "You'll be sorry.
I told you you'd make more mistakes, and this is one right now.
Maybe the biggest you'll ever make."

"Maybe," I said. "But it's the choice I made. See how I did
that? If it looks funny, it's because you've probably never seen me
make one that wasn't subject to your approval before." I blinked at
her. "Now get out of here, before I slap these handcuffs on you
and give Old Man Winter an early Christmas present."

She gave me one last look and turned, walking out unsteady,
gaining strength as she hit her stride, passing Reed and Scott, then
giving Kat only a glance as she walked on out the door.

Chapter 24

I sat in Old Man Winter's office, across from the massive stone desk. I'd slept in my own bed the night before, after Zollers had confirmed to Ariadne that Mormont was the Omega spy. She'd looked oddly relieved, and she had admonished me to get some sleep with a look of mild concern that bordered on motherly, I thought. Or at least my vision of it.

"So it was Mormont all along," Ariadne said, facing the window and staring out. Old Man Winter watched me, his fingers interlaced in front of his face, blocking his mouth. He had returned during the night. "The best way to spy is to be in charge of catching them, I suppose." Ariadne turned from the window and crossed to the desk to stand behind Old Man Winter.

"It was," I said. "Pretty clever, if you're into devious schemes. He plants evidence in my room, sics the vamps on us, gets Andromeda killed—" I frowned at the last, as something wasn't sitting well with me on that one, but I dismissed it.

"He wasn't too kind to you," Ariadne reflected. "Are you sorry to see him dead?"

I felt a flash of regret as I imagined him bleeding, lying on the floor of the practice room. "A little relieved I didn't have to do it myself, I guess."

Old Man Winter raised an eyebrow at that, but Ariadne nodded. "You'll need to go to Dr. Zollers at some point over the next few days—"

"For a de-stressing, yeah," I said with a casual shake of my shoulders. "I know. I'll schedule it. I'm okay, though, really."

Ariadne's eyes shuffled downward. "We haven't talked about

the fact that you spent some time in a cell at our behest recently."

"Yeah." I felt myself tense. "Pretty sure that's some sort of OSHA violation."

"Agreed," Ariadne said, and raised her head. "But we'd like to…try to make it up to you."

I smirked. "Why? Are you afraid I'd sue you? It's not my style, and the court case would be thrown out on the grounds that people with metahuman abilities are a totally ludicrous concept to any sane, normal person."

"All the same," she said, "we're making a large deposit into your bank account with your next check as a minor effort at restitution. And you have our apologies." She waited, as if holding her breath to see what I'd say.

I stared at her, then Old Man Winter. "Is that all?"

I caught a flash of surprise from her, a slight recoil. He, on the other hand, did not react visibly save for his hand, which went to a file laying on his desk, which he slid, very slowly, toward me, as though offering it. I reached out without breaking eye contact and slid it in front of me. I opened the folder and found a piece of paper, typed, the print set like a transcript. As my eyes slid down the page I leaned forward, taking in every detail, starting with the date at the top of the page. I furrowed my brow – it was the date I first came to the Directorate.

[Operator]: Carringer Institute, Minneapolis campus.

[unidentified female]: I need to – dammit [unintelligible] – I need to speak with Erich Winter.

[Operator]: I'm sorry, we don't have anyone listed by that name—

[unidentified female]: Listen to me, I know he's there, that you're a cover for the Directorate. Get me Erich Winter. Tell him it's an emergency, that if I don't speak with him, a metahuman girl will die.

[Operator]: [pause] One moment, please.

[Winter]: Who am I speaking with?

[unidentified female]: You know who I am, Jotun. You've been looking for me for eighteen years.

[Winter]: [pause] Sierra.

[Sierra]: Looks like you're still on top of your game, even a hundred-plus years after Peshtigo.

[Winter]: Why are you calling?

[Sierra]: My daughter. I have a daughter. She's seventeen and Wolfe is after her. He's closing in on her as we speak.

[Winter]: Why do you call me, then?

[Sierra]: Because I can't stop him, dammit. Because I can't get her away. [pause] But you can.

[Winter]: And she is—

[Sierra]: A meta, yes. She's at 832 Hamilton Ave. in Minneapolis. She's...locked in. She can't get out. If he finds her first...

[Winter]: You expect me to throw my men into danger to save her?

[Sierra]: She'll die if you don't.

[Winter]: [pause] I will send agents immediately. If you are lying—

[Sierra]: I'm not.

[Winter]: We still have unfinished business, you and I.

[Sierra]: Not today, Winter. I'm not even in Minnesota anymore. You might want to hurry; you haven't got much time.

[call ends]

I looked up, caught his frozen eyes again, boring into me. "She called you herself. That's how you knew to send Kurt and Zack to get me."

He nodded almost imperceptibly. "She and I...have a somewhat tangled history after the Agency. To send you my way, her need must have been dire."

I stiffened. "Or she just didn't care at all. If you were...enemies, as it were, she put me into your open arms and never so much as checked to see if I was okay."

"I don't believe that is so," he said, motionless.

"Yeah, well," I shook my shoulders lightly, "you didn't live with her as long as I did." I blinked. "She mentioned something. Something coming, a crisis for metas. She called it a storm."

Old Man Winter cocked his head and leaned forward for the first time since I had known him. "Interesting. Did she share any details of this…storm…with you?"

"Nothing specific," I said with a shake of the head. "Just told me it would realign the world of metas, leave us in wreckage."

He settled back into his chair, and Ariadne stared over his shoulder at me, intrigued. "That's not foreboding at all," she said with a frown.

"Sorry. All I've got."

"All right," Ariadne said. "Well…thank you for being so understanding…about everything. Is there…um…anything else you'd like to ask us, or…talk about?" She said it with such concern, I thought she was going to wilt in front of me.

"Nope," I said lightly. "I think it's time for me to get some breakfast, anyway." I stood and looked at the two of them, and then at Ariadne, who actually was wearing a red blouse. "You look nice," I told her. "You should wear color more often."

She blinked at me. "Uhm. Thanks?"

"You're welcome," I said with a smile I felt through the totality of me and walked out, making my way through the rows of cubicles between me and the elevator. I passed the outline of a familiar head and paused in the middle of one of the rows, turning my head sideways to look at the back of a black muss of hair. "J.J.?" I asked, tilting to look at the cubicle dweller hunched over a computer.

He twisted at the waist to turn, his black glasses slipping down his nose as he looked up at me. "Oh. You. How's it going?"

"Good," I said, taking a step into his cubicle. "Did you have as much fun in confinement as I did?"

He blinked, a little dumbstruck. "Um. No. I was bored, man. I thought I was gonna lose it staring at those square walls." He smiled. "Thanks for getting me out."

I waved him off. "Wasn't me. Mormont confessed in front of Zollers and everything; all we did was repeat his story for Ariadne and she was all forgive-y and stuff. Did she try and buy you off with money?"

He pushed his glasses up back to the bridge of his nose. "Yeah. When I saw how much it was I almost asked her to lock me up again...but I was afraid I'd never get the damned squares on the walls out of my head." He straightened. "Do you know how many one foot by one foot squares there were in that place? S—"

"Six hundred," I said, bored. "Yeah." I caught sight of something on the monitor behind him. "Whatcha watching?"

He blushed. "Oh. Uh. That. Well, it's—"

I stepped closer and saw security camera footage of the practice room. I tried to visualize where the camera would have been positioned in order to capture the scene from that angle, and realized I'd never seen any cameras in that room, nor in the Directorate in general. I stared. Mormont was front and center, one hand on the taser, leads still running to my mother, his other holding a gun pointed at me. Visible in the bottom left corner was me, kneeling next to Mom, and Doc Zollers was in the top right, almost ready to fire on Mormont.

"Please don't tell anyone," J.J. said, almost begging. "I just...wanted to see how it happened. I mean," he blushed, "I'm still a little raw at Mormont, if you know what I mean."

"I know what you mean," I said, concentrating on the screen. "Is this video or stillframe?"

"Video." He pushed a button on the keyboard and the picture started to move. Zollers fired and Mormont reacted to the impact of the bullets, falling to the ground. J.J. blushed again. "Please don't tell anyone."

"I won't tell anyone you're watching a snuff film," I said, frowning at the display. "Though that is a little creepy." I looked at Zollers standing there, gun in hand. "Can you rewind?"

"Huh?" He looked at me blankly. "Oh, sure. You want to watch it again?" He let a little half-smile show. "I've watched it like twenty times myself."

I stared at him, mouth slightly open and my eyes crinkled in disgust. "Ew. No. I want you to rewind and show me where Zollers came from. Are there other cameras?"

He turned back to the computer, his face scarlet. "Yeah, yeah, just gimme a…" His fingers danced across the keys and we were treated to a shot of the hallway of the training center, and Dr. Zollers walking backward in rewind, then J.J. changed cameras again and we saw him walk out the front door. The cameras followed him. They were planted all over the Directorate, as we traced his path backward across the lawn and to his office, where a camera caught him sitting alone in front of his desk. I watched the time roll back a minute, then two, as he sat there, seeming to stare off into space. "What's he doing?" J.J. muttered under his breath, and he pushed a button, letting the picture return to the normal flow of time.

"Looks like he's just sitting there," I said, watching him. He had a simple rolltop desk, pushed against the wall – no computer, just Dr. Zollers, sitting, head resting with his fingers against his temples. "Would he know about the cameras?"

"Uh, no," J.J. said, "and neither should you. I mean, don't get me wrong, I'm glad I've got some leverage on the bosses, but let's not push this thing, okay? Don't tell them I showed you this."

"My lips are stapled shut," I said, watching Zollers on the screen. I watched as his hands left his temples and he reached into his desk drawer and pulled out a gun.

"That's weird," J.J. said as I stopped leaning over his shoulder and stood up over him, a cold chill running through me. "What's he doing? How did he know to get his gun? I mean, you know, it's like he walked straight to—"

I slipped my hands out of my gloves and balled one of them up, shoving it hard into J.J.'s mouth to keep him from crying out as I pressed my bare hand against his cheek. He made a noise that was lost amidst the chatter of the cubicle rows and I held tight to him until I felt him lose consciousness. I leaned him back in his seat facing the computer and hoped that no one would notice him until later. Much later.

I kept my calm as I left the headquarters building and didn't start running until after I was out the front doors. I jogged across campus, trying to remain calm inside, trying to act like any one of the other people I'd seen run across the campus in the time I'd been there. They did it for their health, though; I was doing it for someone else's.

I walked to the door I had been through a hundred times, a thousand times, it felt like. I opened it and found myself in the quiet waiting room of Doctor Quinton Zollers, M.D. The fish tank bubbled in the corner, a steady stream of noise that I usually found calming when in concert with the wood-paneled walls. I paced across the carpet to the far door and I hesitated before knocking, my hand raised, ready to descend, when a voice came from behind it, muffled, yet clear. Just like the first time.

"Sienna Nealon. Come right in."

I swallowed heavily, reached into my waistband and withdrew the gun hiding there, felt it cool, gripping my hand, and stepped through the door.

Chapter 25

"Hello," Dr. Zollers said once I was in the room, his dark complexion standing out against the blue sky showing through the window behind him. "I've been expecting you."

"I kinda figured that," I said. "You know why, don't you."

His expression was cool, but there was a hint of levity in his eyes. "You suspect."

I nodded. "You're a meta."

"I am." He kept his infuriating calm. "Always have been."

"You're a telepath." The words sounded incredible as they came out.

"Which makes my career in psychiatry all the more fascinating, wouldn't you say?" He smiled, and made his way over to the chair that he always sat in for our sessions. "Why don't you…have a seat?"

"Okay," I said, though I really didn't want to.

"And you don't need that," he said, nodding at the gun in my hand.

"All right," I answered, and started to put it away but hesitated. I felt an internal tension rising, and wanted to scream at myself not to put the gun back in the holster at my back. "Why would I listen to you?" I asked him, my head rising as I looked him in the eyes and felt a slight tremor in my body.

"It's just good manners, really," he said, and I caught a hint of weariness. "And you might consider the fact that I saved your life the other night."

"Why?" I asked, and I felt myself slip my gun back into the holster. "How?"

"I knew Mormont was bent all along," Zollers said calmly, his fingers steepled. "It was proving it without revealing myself that was the problem. You ever try to frame someone for being a traitor? It's not easy, apparently, even when they are. He didn't tend to keep any real evidence on hand, and certainly not for long enough for me to nail him on it. Not without suspicion falling on me, anyway." He let a slight smile crease his face. "And I couldn't have that."

"So..." My mind raced, struggling to put things together. "...you're like some benevolent meta, working to try and help us, protect us from threats like Mormont?"

"Hardly," Zollers said, and the deep tone of his voice, always so soothing, so reassuring, carried enough of something else that it made me worry – just a little. "I work for...another party."

"Omega?" I asked, feeling the chill grow.

"No," he said with little stir. "Omega is a group of toddlers crashing through sandcastles for all their subtlety when compared to my employers." His usual smile was faded, laced with regret. "They're fearsome, the people I work for, and I mean that in the most literal sense of the word. You should be afraid of them. Very afraid."

"Why?" I asked, feeling almost paralyzed. "Omega has been after me since the day I left my house. They've sent Wolfe after me, Henderschott, James, and those vampires—"

"These people are worse," Zollers said without blinking. "And they don't want you alive, like Omega." His voice softened. "They want you dead."

I felt my mouth dry out as I stared at the man I had trusted with as many of my secrets as anyone else. "You were going to kill me that night with Mormont."

"I was supposed to," Zollers said, and I saw a well of emotion within him. "But I couldn't. I couldn't do it." I saw wetness at the corners of his eyes and he bowed his head. "They'll send someone

else," he said, and his eyes came back up, trying to impart serious-
ness to me. "Next time they'll send someone harder, someone who
won't be as subtle. My mission was always infiltration, but they
have worse. Stone killers, most of them, human and meta, and
they won't hesitate. They'll die to kill you, if need be." There was
no smile now, just a haunted look in his eyes.

"They were the ones who killed Andromeda," I breathed.
"You betrayed us to them when she was killed."

He nodded. "You were supposed to die then, too. I should
have known you'd outmaneuver them." He smiled. "They didn't
much care for that, but I warned them that they were underestimat-
ing you. They didn't listen." His smile evaporated. "They're listening now, I promise you that."

I felt my hand slide down to the pistol again, slow, subtle. I
felt my control start to return and the fear start to rise the moment
he admitted to getting Andromeda killed. My hand slipped onto
the gun, and I drew it slowly, no flourish, and I stared at it dully.
"You saved my life."

"Yes," he said simply.

"I'm going to let you go," I said, and I knew somehow that he
had zero influence over my words now, no dominion, "but not because you saved my life." I blinked and felt tears run down my
face. "I'm letting you go because…you're the only person I've
met who ever made me feel…" I blinked again and the whole im-
age of his face was blurred. "…normal. Like I belonged somewhere."

He stood, slowly, and adjusted his sweater vest as he did so.
"I appreciate that you've made the choice to let me walk. You
were always going to let me go, but you made this decision yourself, without me having to use my power to influence it in the direction I wanted. For that, I'm going to tell you something." He
looked reluctant. "A warning. I don't know if you'll believe me,
but here it is." He took a step closer and placed both hands on my

shoulders, looking deep into my eyes. "Don't trust anyone." He looked at me with those eyes, and I stared back. "No one is looking out for you."

With that, he broke free of me, and started toward the door. I kept the gun trained on his back as he retreated, and he paused at the door to turn back, his hand on the handle.

"Where will you go?" I asked, not sure why I even cared, or if I expected any kind of answer.

"Far," he said. "As far as I can go. There is a storm coming, and the people I work for – worked for – are the heart of it. They'll know I've failed, and they'll want to kill me." He smiled sadly. "And they probably will, eventually, but I'll give them a merry chase before they do." He straightened. "Take care, Sienna Nealon. You are…one of the most unique…" His voice drifted off, and he smiled. "…souls I've ever known."

I watched him carefully. "Worth dying for?"

The ghost of a smile crossed his lips. "Apparently so." He waved a hand at my head. "They'll be along for you in a bit – long after I'm gone, I assure you. Until then," he said, receding from my vision as things started to get blurry, "have a nice nap. It'll make things easier on you if they don't know you let me get away."

"Thank you," I murmured as I curled up on the floor, oddly comforted, as I had been so many times in this office – and now, never would be again.

Chapter 26

"Another cryptic warning," Ariadne said. I sat dazed, in her office, a few hours after Zollers had left. She stared across the desk at me, dour. "You should have warned us before going after him," she said, clenching the pen in her hand. "Instead of—"

"Knocking out J.J. with my powers and rushing off to confront him myself?" I stared straight ahead at her, surprisingly free of emotion. I was weary, even after my nap. "Yeah, I should have. Sorry." I rubbed my face, letting my glove rub against my skin, the soft leather all the comfort I could find at the moment.

"That's going to cost us some more money with J.J.," she said with a sigh. "And Zollers didn't give you a name for his employer? Nothing?"

I shook my head. "Storm. Worse than Omega. Trying to kill me." I shrugged. "Those are the highlights." I could feel my countenance darken. "And they killed Andromeda. On purpose, by the way he told it."

"But why?" Ariadne chewed on the cap of her pen. "Omega wanted her back alive, and this other group wanted her – and you – dead. Why?"

I sat there for a few minutes, quiet, letting it seep in between us. "That is the sixty-four thousand dollar question, isn't it."

She frowned. "The…what? Why sixty-four thousand?"

I felt my face slacken. "It was a show. You should know – you're old. It's an old show."

Her eyebrows creased and turned downward at a forty-five degree angle as her mouth opened in outrage. "How old do you think I am?"

"Not old enough to have watched the Sixty-Four Thousand Dollar Question, apparently."

I was out of her office a few minutes later. I knew she'd tell Old Man Winter everything, but I didn't want to wait to hash it over again; I'd had enough. Also, I was starving, having been forced by Zollers to sleep through breakfast after not eating much of anything yesterday.

The sun was high in the sky, beating down with an intensity that reminded me of the week before, when I'd been searching the Wisconsin woods for an Omega installation. It was overpowering, and even in the short walk from headquarters to the dormitory building, my pores opened and I started to sweat. The smell of the grass was in the air, heavy in the heat. I was thankful as I passed through the doors into the building and felt the sweet relief of the air conditioner.

The smell of food caught me as I walked into the cafeteria. It was beautiful, wonderful, the heavy aroma of onions smelling like a feast. I could hear the chatter from the early lunch crowd and I could almost taste the food as I walked to get my tray. I caught the first dirty look seconds later. A lot of hard glares, I realized as I took myself through the line and got another one from the cafeteria lady who splattered gravy aggressively across my mashed potatoes and onto the tray. I took it back from her, staring at the streak that cut a path across the red tray, like brown blood.

I finished in the line, having reached a point where I was ready to slap the hell out of the next person who gave me a sour expression, and I realized that I was facing something else I didn't want to: the cafeteria was near full, tables occupied from corner to corner.

I sighed, and looked for a friendly face, any friendly face. I was not even close to seeing any; it was as though hostility was drenched over everyone in sight, and the moment I paused to scan the cafeteria after leaving the line, a hush fell and every head turned to me. I stared at them, they stared at me, and I can't recall a time when I wasn't being attacked that I had ever felt so uncomfortable in my life.

"Sienna," I heard someone say over the crowd. Reed waved at me from a table in the distance, and I breathed a sigh of relief as I headed toward him. When I got closer, I realized he wasn't alone – Scott and Kat sat across from him, and a seat was waiting, already pushed out as though it had been readied just for me.

"Tough room," I said as I sat. "Whose cornflakes did I unwittingly pee in?" I looked at the three of them, but with the exception of Kat, who made a face and looked down to her food, I got no reaction. "Seriously, guys, what did I do? Everyone hates me."

"Well," Scott began, "it's not so much any one thing. It's more a...combination of things."

I waited for him to go on, and when he didn't, I sighed and stabbed my fork into the turkey with excessive violence. "Don't be shy," I said, "just say it."

"Well," Scott went on, "you did get perp walked in front of everybody by Clary, and a rumor went around that you were involved with all the agents dying—"

"Are you freaking kidding me?" I said in disbelief. "I—"

"I'm just telling you," Scott said. "I don't believe it, and I've certainly tried to spread the truth, but...it's bad." He hesitated, and I could see the regret on his face. "Really bad."

"They think I...what? Killed agents myself, with my bare hands?" I looked at the three of them, and once again, Scott was the only one to speak.

"The rumor was that you were the traitor," Scott said. "And when Zollers killed Mormont, everyone kind of took a breath and thought for a minute maybe you weren't. But then it turned out Zollers was a traitor too, and you let him get away..."

"Plus, you hurt J.J. and you let your mom walk, too," Kat added. "Apparently a lot of people were pissed at her for kidnapping me, and thought she should have been punished for it." She froze, and her face went white. "Not me, of course; I've been defending you to anyone who will listen, but..." She looked reluctant. "Nobody's listening. Not to us, anyway."

"Great." I tossed my fork onto the plate, not hungry anymore. "Just great."

"Also," Reed said, and I turned toward him, "people heard about you breaking up with Zack and then—"

"Oh. My. God." I said it while holding my hands over my face. "You're not even from here."

"Which probably gives you an idea of how pervasive these rumors are," he said, hesitant. "I don't understand it, personally, because he's a douche, but apparently people really like this Zack guy you broke up with. And then proceeded to cheat on."

"I didn't cheat on him!" I bowed my head. "I didn't actually do anything; I mean we didn't..." I looked at Kat. "You know! You were there, you stopped me!"

Kat shrugged. "Once again...no one's listening. They're saying you slept with the guy from Omega, that you betrayed Zack and the Directorate and all for...uh..." She blushed. "...sexy time."

I was beyond mortified. I wanted to cry right there, but part of me wanted to laugh at the utter absurdity of it all, that I would go through hell to try and make things better, and still the crap could not help but fall upon the fan and blow squarely back into my face.

Reed must have sensed my despair, because I felt his hand on my shoulder, and he gave me a supportive squeeze. "Sorry, uh...sis."

I peaked from behind my fingers. "That's just weird."

"Oh, well," he said, sounding mildly embarrassed, "I don't have to say it anymore. I just thought—"

"No," I said, "it's fine. I like it; it's just..." I took a deep breath. "It might take some getting used to." I looked squarely at him. "Brother." I felt a twinge of oddness as I said it, a feeling that settled as I rolled it over in my head again. "Brother."

He broke into an easy smile. "I've been waiting to hear you say that for kind of a long while."

"Maybe you should have told me earlier, then...like when I first climbed into your car and pointed a gun at you."

"Are you kidding?" He raised an eyebrow as he smiled at me and took a bite of a chicken nugget. "You had a gun. You might have shot me."

I laughed, somehow, in spite of it all, and I heard Kat and Scott join me a moment later. I held my head in my hands, felt the soft leather on them. It was comforting again, that old familiar feeling, but something different, too, and soothing in its own way. Surrounded by a bunch of hostile people in the cafeteria at large, but the ones close by weren't hostile at all. I looked from Scott, his wide grin and face flushed red from laughing to Kat, her tanned and pretty cheerleader look, her eyes riveted on Scott as he let out another peel of laughter, and she joined him.

I turned then to Reed. He wore a grin of his own, his long dark hair hanging back in a ponytail, swept over his shoulder. I smiled at them, at the thought of them, actually, and I laughed again, against all odds. After a moment I stopped. "You're going to tell me about him, right? About...Dad?"

"Absolutely," Reed said with a nod and a half-smile of his own. "Anything you want to know."

"Mind if I join you all?" I turned at the sound of the voice, and my jaw dropped more than slightly, my eyes fluttering in surprise. Zack walked up with his tray supported in his hands, a neutral look on his face.

I turned back to the table, and met the three of them looking to me, and realized that the decision was mine. "Have a seat," I said, and nodded at him.

He turned and pulled an empty chair from a nearby table, and slid it up to sit next to me with a nod to everyone else. "How are you holding up?" he asked.

I thought about it. My mouth came open, and a million responses, both probable and improbable, threatened to fall out, every one of them carrying far more detail than was actually needed. "I'm…" I blinked, and a thousand more ran through my mind before I settled on one that came out. "I'm good," I said, and I wondered if it was true. I thought for a second, and decided it was, or as close to it as was possible at this stage in my life. "I'm good. How are you?"

He chewed on a french fry, and averted his gaze. "Not as good as you, it sounds like."

"Well," I said, swallowing a bite of food, "it's a tall order to fill, you know, what with all the awesome life events I've experienced lately…"

He broke a slight smile at that one. "Sure. Tons of fun stuff has happened, right?"

"Exactly," I said, nodding. "Lots of big stuff. Crazy stuff. Like, I have a brother." I reached back and slapped Reed on the shoulder. He looked up from his meal, surprise turning to annoyance from my slap.

"I heard about that. Well, I'm glad it's all been going good," Zack said, and paused, searching my eyes for something.

"Not all of it," I amended. "There are some things that haven't been so fun." I lowered my voice a notch. "Some things I regret, if you know what I mean. Things I'm…sorry about."

I caught the flicker in his expression, the subtle nod. "Yeah. I've…had one of those myself." He cleared his throat. "I hate regrets."

"Me too," I agreed. I tried to smile, and did. "I don't really like having regrets. I tend to like to…resolve things, if I can."

"Me too," he said with a shake of the head. "What do you do about something like that? You know, to resolve it?"

I took a deep breath and pretended to think about it. "You know...I think it depends on what the wronged party wants to do. For my part...I'm sorry."

I thought I caught a little relief, and he nodded. "Me too. Things happened...that I wish had never happened. And...if I could have anything I wanted, it'd be to go back to the way things were before."

"Really?" I raised an eyebrow at him. "Even after...everything?"

"Yeah," he said finally, after clearing his throat again. "Because...'everything'...isn't as bad as...what would happen if..." He looked up, as though trying to straighten out what he was trying to say in his head. "Oh, geez, I just..." He met my eyes, and his hand reached out for mine, and I felt his hands take mine, watched his bare skin stroke against the leather of my glove. "The physical isn't everything to me. I just want to go back to the way things were."

"You sure?" I waited, and he nodded. "I wouldn't mind that either, because...you're right. It's not. But going back to the way things were is a better deal for me than you, so...yeah. I'll take it. And...I really am sorry."

"I know," he said, and he looked me in the eye as he said it.

"Wait..." Kat said, staring at the two of us with squinted eyes, "did you two just get back together? Is that what that was?" She blinked twice. "No, really. I honestly have no idea."

Reed laughed, followed by Scott, and then Zack. Kat finally let out a little guffaw of her own, and I started to join them but stopped. I was here, in my little oasis, hostile people all around, but my friends closest, surrounding me.

And yet Zollers' last words, his warning, came back to me, and as they laughed, the sound was cold to my ears, and I was alone in the midst of them all. I felt those little hairs on the back of my neck tingle, the nerves firing off one by one, as the laughter grew at the table around me. I felt the feeling fade, and slowly, painfully slow, I let a smile spread across my face as I put that thought out of my mind.

A Note to the Reader

I wanted to take a moment to thank you for reading this story. As an independent author, getting my name out to build an audience is one of the biggest priorities on any given day. If you enjoyed this story and are looking forward to reading more, let someone know - post it on Amazon, on your blog, if you have one, on Goodreads.com, place it in a quick Facebook status or Tweet with a link to the page of whatever outlet you purchased it from (Amazon, Barnes & Noble, Apple, Kobo, etc). Good reviews inspire people to take a chance on a new author – like me. And we new authors can use all the help we can get.

Thanks again for your time.

Robert J. Crane

About the Author

Robert J. Crane was born and raised on Florida's Space Coast before moving to the upper midwest in search of cooler climates and more palatable beer. He graduated from the University of Central Florida with a degree in English Creative Writing. He worked for a year as a substitute teacher and worked in the financial services field for seven years while writing in his spare time. He makes his home in the Twin Cities area of Minnesota.

He can be contacted in several ways:
Via **email** at cyrusdavidon@gmail.com
Follow him on **Twitter** - @robertJcrane
Connect on **Facebook** – robertJcrane (Author)
Website – http://www.robertJcrane.com
Blog – http://robertJcrane.blogspot.com
Become a fan on **Goodreads** –
http://www.goodreads.com/RobertJCrane

Sienna Nealon will return in

OMEGA
THE GIRL IN THE BOX, BOOK FIVE

Omega – a shadowy organization that is synonomous with power in the metahuman world. They have hunted Sienna Nealon since the day she first left her house, killed countless Directorate agents and operatives, and now they unveil their greatest plot – Operation Stanchion, a phrase whispered to Sienna by an Omega operative almost too scared to speak the words aloud. Now Sienna must track the pieces Omega has in motion, journeying across the upper midwest to confront the forces that have plagued her since she first stepped into the metahuman world before they can land their final stroke – and bring an end to the Directorate forever.

Coming Early 2013

The Sanctuary Series
Epic Fantasy by Robert J. Crane

The world of Arkaria is a dangerous place, filled with dragons, titans, goblins and other dangers. Those who live in this world are faced with two choices: live an ordinary life or become an adventurer and seek the extraordinary.

Defender
The Sanctuary Series, Volume One
Cyrus Davidon leads a small guild in the human capital of Reikonos. Caught in an untenable situation, facing death in the den of a dragon, they are saved by the brave fighters of Sanctuary who offer an invitation filled with the promise of greater adventure. Soon Cyrus is embroiled in a mystery - someone is stealing weapons of nearly unlimited power for an unknown purpose, and Sanctuary may be the only thing that stands between the world of Arkaria and total destruction.

Available Now!

Avenger
The Sanctuary Series, Volume Two
When a series of attacks on convoys draws suspicion that Sanctuary is involved, Cyrus Davidon must put aside his personal struggles and try to find the raiders. As the attacks worsen, Cyrus and his comrades find themselves abandoned by their allies, surrounded by enemies, facing the end of Sanctuary and a war that will consume their world.

Available Now!

Champion
The Sanctuary Series, Volume Three

As the war heats up in Arkaria, Vara is forced to flee after an ancient order of skilled assassins infiltrates Sanctuary and targets her. Cyrus Davidon accompanies her home to the elven city of Termina and the two of them become embroiled in a mystery that will shake the very foundations of the Elven Kingdom – and Arkaria.

Available Now!

Crusader
The Sanctuary Series, Volume Four

Cyrus Davidon finds himself far from his home in Sanctuary, in the land of Luukessia, a place divided and deep in turmoil. With his allies at his side, Cyrus finds himself facing off against an implacable foe in a war that will challenge all his convictions - and one he may not be able to win.

Coming Early 2013!

Savages
A Sanctuary Short Story

Twenty years before Cyrus Davidon joined Sanctuary, his father was killed in a war with the trolls and he has never forgiven them. Enter Vaste, a troll unlike most; courageous, loyal and an outcast. When Cyrus and Vaste become trapped in a far distant land, they are forced to overcome their suspicions and work together to get home.

Available Now!

A Familiar Face
A Sanctuary Short Story

Cyrus Davidon gets more than he bargained for when he takes a day away from Sanctuary to visit the busy markets of his hometown, Reikonos. While there, he meets a woman who seems very familiar, and appears to know him, but that he can't place.

Available Now!

The Girl in the Box
Contemporary Urban Fantasy by Robert J. Crane

Alone
The Girl in the Box, Book 1

Sienna Nealon was a 17 year-old girl who had been held prisoner in her own house by her mother for twelve years. Then one day her mother vanished, and Sienna woke up to find two strange men in her home. On the run, unsure of who to turn to and discovering she possesses mysterious powers, Sienna finds herself pursued by a shadowy agency known as the Directorate and hunted by a vicious, bloodthirsty psychopath named Wolfe, each of which is determined to capture her for their own purposes...

Available Now!

Untouched
The Girl in the Box, Book 2

Still haunted by her last encounter with Wolfe and searching for her mother, Sienna Nealon must put aside her personal struggles when a new threat emerges – Aleksandr Gavrikov, a metahuman so powerful, he could destroy entire cities – and he's focused on bringing the Directorate to its knees.

Available Now!

Soulless
The Girl in the Box, Book 3

After six months of intense training with the Directorate, Sienna Nealon finds herself on her first assignment – tracking a dangerous meta across the upper midwest. With Scott Byerly and Kat Forrest at her side, she'll face new enemies and receive help from unlikely allies as she stumbles across the truth behind the shadowy organization known only as Omega.

Available Now!

CPSIA information can be obtained
at www.ICGtesting.com
Printed in the USA
LVOW01s2350040416
482093LV00030B/1285/P